Notting Hill Editions is an independent British publisher. The company was founded by Tom Kremer (1930–2017), champion of innovation and the man responsible for popularising the Rubik's Cube.

After a successful business career in toy invention Tom decided, at the age of eighty, to fulfil his passion for literature. In a fast-moving digital world Tom's aim was to revive the art of the essay, and to create exceptionally beautiful books that would be lingered over and cherished.

Hailed as 'the shape of things to come', the family-run press brings to print the most surprising thinkers of past and present. In an era of information-overload, these collectible pocket-size books distil ideas that linger in the mind.

Stephen Johnson is the author of two books, *How Shostakovich Changed My Mind*, also published by Notting Hill Editions, and *The Eighth: Mahler and the World in 1910*, published by Faber in 2020. He has taken part in several hundred radio programmes and documentaries, including BBC Radio 3's weekly Discovering Music series, and has made numerous appearances on TV, contributing as a guest interviewee on BBC Radio 4's coverage of The Proms, ITV's *The South Bank Show*, and on BBC1's *The One Show*. Additionally, he made an important contribution, both as commentator and narrator, to Tony Palmer's controversial film about the composer Ralph Vaughan Williams, *Oh Thou Transcendent*, and more recently to Palmer's film about Gustav Holst, *In the Bleak Midwinter*. Stephen is also a composer and his clarinet quintet Angel's Arc had three performances in the UK in 2019, and will premiere in New York in November 2021. His new string quartet will premiere in the UK in November 2021.

THE WRONG TURNING

Encounters with Ghosts

–

Introduced and Edited by
Stephen Johnson

 Notting Hill Editions

133.1

First Published in 2021
by Notting Hill Editions Ltd
Mirefoot, Burneside, Kendal LA8 9AB

Series design by FLOK Design, Berlin, Germany
Cover design by Plain Creative, Kendal
Creative Advisor: Dennis PAPHITIS

Typeset by CB Editions, London
Printed and bound by Gutenberg Press Ltd, Malta

Cover illustration: Outremonde (litho) by Jean Chaintrier
Copyright © ADAGP, Paris and DACS, London 2021
Photo copyright © J.P. Zenobel / Bridgeman Images

A CIP record for this book is available from the British Library

ISBN 978-1-912559-30-5

nottinghilleditions.com

One need not be a Chamber – to be Haunted –
One need not be a House –
The Brain has Corridors – surpassing
Material Place –

Far safer, of a Midnight Meeting
External Ghost
Than its interior Confronting –
That Cooler Host [. . .]

The Body – borrows a Revolver –
He bolts the Door –
O'erlooking a superior spectre –
Or More –

– Emily Dickinson, '670', *c.*1863

Contents

Stephen Johnson

– Introduction –

'A menacing enchantment' – that memorable phrase occurs in *The Sculptor's Daughter*, the childhood memoir of Tove Jansson, creator of the Moomins. It captures the sense of both magic and encroaching darkness that was so much part of the infant (and adult) Jansson's imaginative world. And yet there was one thing that made little Tove feel safe amid the blackness of the long Finnish winter nights: stories, particularly the stories told to her by her mother, the illustrator Signe Hammarsten-Jansson – later the model for Jansson's wise, practical, endlessly loving Moominmamma:

The log-fire is alight and we draw up the big chair. We turn out the lights in the studio and sit in front of the fire and she says: once there was a little girl who was terribly pretty and her mummy liked her so awfully much . . . A soft gentle voice in the warm darkness and one gazes into the fire and nothing is dangerous. Everything else is outside and can't get in. Not now or at any time.

But not everyone is blessed with a mummy like Signe-Hammarsten-Jansson. For those who aren't, there may be another possibility: that the story itself can perform a similar function, giving form to the threatening shadows, and in the process taming them, containing them. When the story is well told, maybe the very pleasure we take in the telling can help us deal with those fears – make them less menacing and more enchanting.

My first memory of being gripped, scared, but also enthralled, by a ghost story goes back to when I was about five. I was with my mother in the kitchen, and David Davis, head of BBC's *Children's Hour*, was beginning a story on the radio. I'd heard that beautifully modulated, deliciously reassuring voice before, reading *Winnie the Pooh* and *The Wind in the Willows*, and I made myself comfortable in preparation for a similar 'Listen with Mother' session. What I got, however, was M. R. James's terrifying *The Haunted Doll's House*, in which two children are somehow made away with by the hideous, frog-faced apparition of the rich grandfather their coldly avaricious parents have obviously murdered. I remember spending a fearful, truly haunted night – and yet I was also hooked. Was this pure emotional masochism on my part, or was there a sense that I needed to face something down? To peer into the darkness that so frightened me? Could it even be that I'd begun to realise what Thomas Hardy had grasped: that, 'If a way to the better there be, it exacts a full look at the worst'?

After decades of grappling with the dread and

weird exhilaration that goes with the bipolar condition I have suffered with since my teens, I'd like to think that I was close to the right track. Human beings have always loved frightening and being frightened by each other – within reason, of course, and as long as one retains that sense of being in a fundamentally 'safe space'. An adrenaline rush, followed by a pleasurable dopamine release when one draws oneself up, looks around, and remembers that it's all make-believe – maybe for many that's all it ever needs to be. But for others, and especially for some of the troubled men and women who wove these stories together in the first place, I suspect that it was more than that. Looking back on the ghost stories that riveted me as a teenager and as a young adult, I'm struck by how many of them contain descriptions of states of mind strongly reminiscent of my own more unpleasant episodes. Picture M. R. James's unfortunate scholar Dunning, in *Casting the Runes*, on his way back from the solidly rational British Museum to his reassuringly dull suburban dwelling place, unaware that a curse has been placed upon him:

More than once on his way home that day Mr. Dunning confessed to himself that he did not look forward with his usual cheerfulness to a solitary evening. It seemed to him that something ill-defined and impalpable had stepped between him and his fellow-men – had taken him in charge, as it were.

3

Excursions into dangerous mental territory often start with something like that. As James says in one of the stories included here, 'Oh, Whistle, and I'll Come to You, My Lad', *experto crede* – 'believe one who has experience of this.' That flash of personal detail, rare in James's stories, has led some to infer that the author himself had encountered appalling supernatural events like those he describes so vividly. But James always denied it, and I believe him. The experience I think he alludes to is the mental state itself: terror, painfully heightened awareness (hypervigilance, as the specialists put it) and dreadful imaginings – half-waking nightmares beyond the conscious control of the sufferer. I have experienced the same kind of thing myself at times when I've sensed, however falteringly, however unwillingly, that I too was contending with something that occupied the haunted corridors of my own brain: something too dreadful to be faced directly. It's striking how many of the finest, subtlest ghost stories leave open the question of whether the 'ghost' is best understood as an objective or a subjective horror – Emily Dickinson's 'superior spectre'. Henry James's classic *The Turn of the Screw* springs to mind, followed speedily and stealthily by Charlotte Perkins Gilman's taut little masterpiece *The Yellow Wallpaper*. Penelope's Lively's *Black Dog* poses the same question, but the other way round: initially it seems likely that the disturbance is 'all in the mind'; but could it actually be objectively real – or is there another, still more challenging way of looking at it? The best ghost stories often leave the reader with questions like that, questions which, however plausibly they may be answered, only lead to more questions: in Dickinson's words, 'a superior spectre – Or More – '?

Therein lies the big difference between the ghost story and the other great English-language mystery genre, the detective story. Many detective stories start by creating a sense of the uncanny, so much so that we may at first believe there really is an element of the supernatural – think of Conan Doyle's *The Hound of the Baskervilles*, Agatha Christie's *The Pale Horse*, or any number of G. K. Chesterton's Father Brown stories. Then the detective gets to work; reason is applied and finally light is shone into those dark corners. Bewildering, frightening events are explained and set in order – think how many of these expertly engineered tales end with the triumphant sleuth laying it all out in clear narrative form to an enthralled audience. The rational mind – what Poirot famously called his 'little grey cells' – has triumphed.

Great ghost stories rarely start by springing the traumatic event upon us; more usually they build up to it steadily, carefully, though we may sense early on that something is seriously amiss, even – perhaps especially – when the scene set before us at the outset appears comfortable, predictable, everyday. It can be solid, orderly and well-lit as Mr. Dunning's British Museum, or cosy as the family fireside setting where W. W. Jacobs's

'The Monkey's Paw' begins its steady crescendo of horror. We are lulled into a false sense of security, and so are less able to dismiss or diminish the terrible thing when it finally reveals itself.

For Robert Aickman, the still undervalued creator of what he preferred to call 'strange stories', there was a lot more to all this than the enjoyment of a little adrenalin-boosting fun. Aickman set out his theory in a letter he wrote on his acceptance of the World Fantasy Award in 1976:

I believe that at the time of the Industrial and French Revolutions . . . mankind took a wrong turning. The beliefs that one day, by application of reason and the scientific method, everything will be known, and every problem and unhappiness solved, seem to me to have led to a situation where, first, we are in imminent danger of destroying the whole world.

Whatever one thinks of Aickman's comments as a philosophical or historical summary – an explanation of where humankind as a whole went astray – the notion of some kind of 'wrong turning' does seem to lie behind a lot of the most enduring literary ghost stories. No matter whether it involves a literal wrong turning or something more mysterious and elusive, in each case a character makes a mistake and places trust in the wrong kind of mental compass: nemesis is waiting in the wings to punish hubris. Something within us, the 'superior spectre', needs to be encountered and reckoned with, and when we meet it, Poirot's little grey cells aren't adequate to deal with it on their own. Whether what we confront in the haunted chamber is the Freudian 'return of the repressed', the Jungian 'shadow' self, the embodiment of some buried childhood trauma or simply a personification of the terrible fact of death (for M. R. James, the 'King of Terrors'), to come to terms with what the ghost represents we must expand our mental horizons. If we are to achieve fully integrated minds, we can't go on being left-brain supremacists, insisting on the primacy of analytic language, scientific logic and objective truth: we must accept that the right hemisphere of the brain, with its resources of fantasy, poetic symbolism and subjective insight, has something vitally important to tell us too. That has certainly been my experience. Looking back over nearly a quarter of a century of serious therapeutic work, I'm struck by how often, in trying to explain my own terrifying mental states to psychiatrists or psychotherapists, I've resorted to images or turns of phrase in some of my own favourite ghost stories. Shakespeare famously spoke of how, 'as imagination bodies forth the forms of things unknown', the poet 'turns them to shapes and gives to airy nothing a local habitation and a name.' The poet, mark you, not the clinician or the neuroscientist: and when, with his or her help, our shadows acquire that shape and that name they somehow become less frightening, more manageable, or at least liveable with.

But not necessarily more rational. A good ghost story remains, in the end, an exercise in what Keats called 'Negative capability': the state of mind in which we are not only able but willing to remain 'in uncertainties, mysteries, doubts, without any irritable reaching after fact and reason'. When it comes to confronting one's own internal horrors that, I believe, is essential. At the end of one of Robert Aickman's finest stories, *Into the Wood*, the central character, Margaret, experiences a classic face-off with her husband, Henry, who – like quite a few of the male characters in these stories – thinks that his wife just needs to 'be reasonable' and everything will return to sane, safe normality:

The argument took every bit as long as she expected, but Margaret was developing new resources now, even though she had little idea what they were.

'I'll let you know immediately I get out of the wood,' she promised. 'It's one of those things you have to live through until you emerge the other side.'

The line between menace and enchantment may be perilously thin, but, on the evidence of these stories, treading it can be as perversely delightful for the writer as for the reader: so often there's a glint of wicked playfulness amid the darkness. The moral and psychological horrors conveyed in *The Turn of the Screw* are real enough, but there's also something teasing at work here, evident in the way James layers ambiguity on ambiguity, creating an Escher-like nest of tables for the would-be interpreter. Something similar flickers in the irony and deft understatement of M.R. James's '*Oh, Whistle, and I'll Come to You, My Lad*', even after the shocking climax – 'as you may imagine, the Professor's views on certain points are less clear than they used to be.' 'I could a tale unfold', says the Ghost in *Hamlet*, 'whose lightest word / Would harrow up thy soul, freeze thy young blood, / Make thy two eyes like stars start from their spheres, / Thy knotted and combined locks to part, / And each particular hair to stand on end / Like quills upon the fretful porpentine.' There's something about that outrageously florid language that suggests that this 'poor ghost' is having a thoroughly good time scaring the morbidly imaginative Prince out of his wits.

As for Flann O'Brien, or, rather, Myles na gCopaleen – best to let him speak for himself, which he does with characteristic brilliance, in the space of a newspaper column, at the end of this collection. I'll just say it turns out that there's more than one way of dealing with superior spectres.

† Granted, Emily Brontë's *Wuthering Heights* is not, in any normal sense, a 'ghost story'; but ghosts do play a significant role in the novel, however brief and shadowy their presences may be. An encounter with a ghost – or at least the possibility of one – is what sets the novel's central narrative in motion, and its ambiguous, hauntingly beautiful coda hinges on the question of whether intense passion and pain cease when the sufferers' earthly lives are over.

A little scene-setting is necessary before our first extract. The prosperous, ever-so-slightly foppish Lockwood has just taken up the tenancy of Thrushcross Grange, a country house in a sheltered valley amongst the wild and desolate Yorkshire Pennines. His curiosity about his new landlord, the sullen, enigmatic Heathcliff, has driven him to seek the latter out, on a snowy winter's day, at his remote farmhouse, Wuthering Heights; and this, it soon becomes clear, is his first significant 'wrong turning'. There Lockwood receives a welcome worthy of the classic TV black comedy, *The League of Gentlemen*. He is harangued by the crabbed-souled, fanatically religious servant Joseph, treated with oddly defensive resentment by the as yet unnamed young woman of the house, and with undisguised hostility by the shabby Hareton. As for Heathcliff, the only thing that forces a smile from him is Lockwood's ineffectual protesting when he's set upon by two enormous guard dogs. With the moors now impassable, and Lockwood bruised and faint from his ordeal, Heathcliff grudgingly orders the servant Zillah to give his guest brandy and find him somewhere to sleep. But for the unfortunate Lockwood, there is worse to come.

10

Emily Brontë

– *from* Wuthering Heights (1847) –

While leading the way upstairs, she recommended that I should hide the candle, and not make a noise; for her master had an odd notion about the chamber she would put me in, and never let anybody lodge there willingly.

I asked the reason.

She did not know, she answered: she had only lived there a year or two; and they had so many queer goings on, she could not begin to be curious.

Too stupefied to be curious myself, I fastened my door and glanced round for the bed. The whole furniture consisted of a chair, a clothes-press, and a large oak case, with squares cut out near the top resembling coach windows.

Having approached this structure, I looked inside, and perceived it to be a singular sort of old-fashioned couch, very conveniently designed to obviate the necessity for every member of the family having a room to himself. In fact, it formed a little closet, and the ledge of a window, which it enclosed, served as a table.

I slid back the panelled sides, got in with my light, pulled them together again, and felt secure against the vigilance of Heathcliff, and every one else.

The ledge, where I placed my candle, had a few mildewed books piled up in one corner; and it was covered with writing scratched on the paint. This writing, however, was nothing but a name repeated in all kinds of characters, large and small – *Catherine Earnshaw*, here and there varied to *Catherine Heathcliff*, and then again to *Catherine Linton*.

In vapid listlessness I leant my head against the window, and continued spelling over Catherine Earnshaw – Heathcliff – Linton, till my eyes closed; but they had not rested five minutes when a glare of white letters started from the dark, as vivid as spectres – the air swarmed with Catherines; and rousing myself to dispel the obtrusive name, I discovered my candle-wick reclining on one of the antique volumes, and perfuming the place with an odour of roasted calf-skin.

I snuffed it off, and, very ill at ease under the influence of cold and lingering nausea, sat up and spread open the injured tome on my knee. It was a Testament, in lean type, and smelling dreadfully musty: a flyleaf bore the inscription – 'Catherine Earnshaw, her book,' and a date some quarter of a century back.

I shut it, and took up another and another, till I had examined all. Catherine's library was select, and its state of dilapidation proved it to have been well used, though not altogether for a legitimate purpose: scarcely one chapter had escaped a pen-and-ink commentary – at least the appearance of one – covering every morsel of blank that the printer had left.

Some were detached sentences; other parts took the form of a regular diary, scrawled in an unformed, childish hand. At the top of an extra page (quite a treasure, probably, when first lighted on) I was greatly amused to behold an excellent caricature of my friend Joseph – rudely, yet powerfully sketched.

An immediate interest kindled within me for the unknown Catherine, and I began forthwith to decipher her faded hieroglyphics.

'An awful Sunday,' commenced the paragraph beneath. 'I wish my father were back again. Hindley is a detestable substitute – his conduct to Heathcliff is atrocious – H. and I are going to rebel – we took our initiatory step this evening.

'All day had been flooding with rain; we could not go to church, so Joseph must needs get up a congregation in the garret; and, while Hindley and his wife basked downstairs before a comfortable fire – doing anything but reading their Bibles, I'll answer for it – Heathcliff, myself, and the unhappy ploughboy were commanded to take our prayer-books, and mount: we were ranged in a row, on a sack of corn, groaning and shivering, and hoping that Joseph would shiver too, so that he might give us a short homily for his own sake. A vain idea! The service lasted precisely three hours; and yet my brother had the face to exclaim, when he saw us descending,

"What, done already?"

'On Sunday evenings we used to be permitted to play, if we did not make much noise; now a mere titter is sufficient to send us into corners.'

[. . .] 'How little did I dream that Hindley would ever make me cry so!' she wrote. 'My head aches, till I cannot keep it on the pillow; and still I can't give over. Poor Heathcliff! Hindley calls him a vagabond, and won't let him sit with us, nor eat with us any more; and, he says, he and I must not play together, and threatens to turn him out of the house if we break his orders.

'He has been blaming our father (how dared he?) for treating H. too liberally; and swears he will reduce him to his right place – '

[. . .] I remembered I was lying in the oak closet, and I heard distinctly the gusty wind, and the driving of the snow; I heard, also, the fir bough repeat its teasing sound, and ascribed it to the right cause: but it annoyed me so much, that I resolved to silence it, if possible; and, I thought, I rose and endeavoured to unhasp the casement. The hook was soldered into the staple: a circumstance observed by me when awake, but forgotten.

'I must stop it, nevertheless!' I muttered, knocking my knuckles through the glass, and stretching an arm out to seize the importunate branch; instead of which, my fingers closed on the fingers of a little, ice-cold hand!

The intense horror of nightmare came over me: I

tried to draw back my arm, but the hand clung to it, and a most melancholy voice sobbed,

'Let me in – let me in!'

'Who are you?' I asked, struggling, meanwhile, to disengage myself.

'Catherine Linton,' it replied, shiveringly (why did I think of *Linton*? I had read *Earnshaw* twenty times for Linton) – 'I'm come home: I'd lost my way on the moor!'

As it spoke, I discerned, obscurely, a child's face looking through the window. Terror made me cruel; and, finding it useless to attempt shaking the creature off, I pulled its wrist on to the broken pane, and rubbed it to and fro till the blood ran down and soaked the bedclothes: still it wailed, 'Let me in!' and maintained its tenacious grip, almost maddening me with fear.

'How can I!' I said at length. 'Let *me* go, if you want me to let you in!'

The fingers relaxed, I snatched mine through the hole, hurriedly piled the books up in a pyramid against it, and stopped my ears to exclude the lamentable prayer.

I seemed to keep them closed above a quarter of an hour; yet, the instant I listened again, there was the doleful cry moaning on!

'Begone!' I shouted. 'I'll never let you in, not if you beg for twenty years.'

'It is twenty years,' mourned the voice: 'twenty years. I've been a waif for twenty years!'

Thereat began a feeble scratching outside, and the pile of books moved as if thrust forward.

I tried to jump up; but could not stir a limb; and so yelled aloud, in a frenzy of fright.

To my confusion, I discovered the yell was not ideal: hasty footsteps approached my chamber door; somebody pushed it open, with a vigorous hand, and a light glimmered through the squares at the top of the bed. I sat shuddering, yet, and wiping the perspiration from my forehead: the intruder appeared to hesitate, and muttered to himself.

At last, he said, in a half-whisper, plainly not expecting an answer,

'Is anyone here?'

I considered it best to confess my presence; for I knew Heathcliff's accents, and feared he might search further, if I kept quiet.

With this intention, I turned and opened the panels. I shall not soon forget the effect my action produced.

Heathcliff stood near the entrance, in his shirt and trousers; with a candle dripping over his fingers, and his face as white as the wall behind him. The first creak of the oak startled him like an electric shock: the light leaped from his hold to a distance of some feet, and his agitation was so extreme, that he could hardly pick it up.

'It is only your guest, sir,' I called out, desirous to spare him the humiliation of exposing his cowardice further. 'I had the misfortune to scream in my sleep, owing to a frightful nightmare. I'm sorry I disturbed you.'

'Oh, God confound you, Mr. Lockwood! I wish you were at the –' commenced my host, setting the candle on a chair, because he found it impossible to hold it steady.

'And who showed you up into this room?' he continued, crushing his nails into his palms, and grinding his teeth to subdue the maxillary convulsions. 'Who was it? I've a good mind to turn them out of the house this moment?'

'It was your servant Zillah,' I replied, flinging myself on to the floor, and rapidly resuming my garments. 'I should not care if you did, Mr. Heathcliff; she richly deserves it. I suppose that she wanted to get another proof that the place was haunted, at my expense. Well, it is – swarming with ghosts and goblins! You have reason in shutting it up, I assure you. No one will thank you for a doze in such a den!'

'What do you mean?' asked Heathcliff, 'and what are you doing? Lie down and finish out the night, since you *are* here; but, for Heaven's sake! don't repeat that horrid noise: nothing could excuse it, unless you were having your throat cut!'

'If the little fiend had got in at the window, she probably would have strangled me!' I returned. 'I'm not going to endure the persecutions of your hospitable ancestors again . . . And that minx, Catherine Linton, or Earnshaw, or however she was called – she must have been a changeling – wicked little soul! She told me she had been walking the earth these twenty years: a just punishment for her mortal transgressions, I've no doubt!'

Scarcely were these words uttered when I recollected the association of Heathcliff's with Catherine's name in the book, which had completely slipped from my memory, till thus awakened. I blushed at my inconsideration: but, without showing further consciousness of the offence, I hastened to add,

'The truth is, sir, I passed the first part of the night in –' Here I stopped afresh – I was about to say 'perusing those old volumes', then it would have revealed my knowledge of their written, as well as their printed, contents; so, correcting myself, I went on,

'In spelling over the name scratched on that window-ledge. A monotonous occupation, calculated to set me asleep, like counting, or –'

'What *can* you mean by talking in this way to *me*!' thundered Heathcliff with savage vehemence. 'How – how *dare* you, under my roof? – God! he's mad to speak so!' And he struck his forehead with rage.

I did not know whether to resent this language or pursue my explanation; but he seemed so powerfully affected that I took pity and proceeded with my dreams; affirming I had never heard the appellation of 'Catherine Linton' before, but reading it often over produced an impression which personified itself when

I had no longer my imagination under control.

Heathcliff gradually fell back into the shelter of the bed, as I spoke; finally sitting down almost concealed behind it. I guessed, however, by his irregular and intercepted breathing, that he struggled to vanquish an excess of violent emotion.

Not liking to show him that I had heard the conflict, I continued my toilette rather noisily, looked at my watch, and soliloquised on the length of the night:

'Not three o'clock yet! I could have taken oath it had been six. Time stagnates here: we must surely have retired to rest at eight!'

'Always at nine in winter, and rise at four,' said my host, suppressing a groan: and, as I fancied, by the motion of his arm's shadow, dashing a tear from his eyes.

'Mr. Lockwood,' he added, 'you may go into my room: you'll only be in the way, coming downstairs so early: and your childish outcry has sent sleep to the devil for me.'

'And for me, too,' I replied. 'I'll walk in the yard till daylight, and then I'll be off; and you need not dread a repetition of my intrusion. I'm now quite cured of seeking pleasure in society, be it country or town. A sensible man ought to find sufficient company in himself.'

'Delightful company!' muttered Heathcliff. 'Take the candle, and go where you please. I shall join you directly. Keep out of the yard, though, the dogs are unchained; and the house – Juno mounts sentinel there, and – nay, you can only ramble about the steps and passages. But, away with you! I'll come in two minutes!'

I obeyed, so far as to quit the chamber; when, ignorant where the narrow lobbies led, I stood still, and was witness, involuntarily, to a piece of superstition on the part of my landlord which belied, oddly, his apparent sense.

He got on to the bed, and wrenched open the lattice, bursting, as he pulled at it, into an uncontrollable passion of tears.

'Come in! Come in!' he sobbed. 'Cathy, do come. Oh, do – *once* more! Oh! My heart's darling! Hear me *this* time, Catherine, at last!'

The spectre showed a spectre's ordinary caprice: it gave no sign of being; but the snow and wind whirled wildly through, even reaching my station, and blowing out the light.

There was such anguish in the gush of grief that accompanied this raving, that my compassion made me overlook its folly, and I drew off, half angry to have listened at all, and vexed at having related my ridiculous nightmare, since it produced that agony; though *why* was beyond my comprehension.

I descended cautiously to the lower regions, and landed in the back-kitchen, where a gleam of fire, raked compactly together, enabled me to rekindle my candle.

✝ One phrase in particular stands out for me on rereading that extract from *Wuthering Heights*: 'Terror made me cruel'. It's one of Brontë's many insights into the murky complexities of the human soul that might well have impressed even the master-psychologist Dostoyevsky.

A ghost story which we know did impress Dostoyevsky – as it did just about every Russian writer of note – was Alexander Pushkin's *The Queen of Spades*, which first appeared in print in 1834, thirteen years before *Wuthering Heights*. Early on we find a classic account of a wrong turning, taken apparently in full consciousness, and for all manner of wrong reasons. Lisaveta is the poor relation of the appalling Countess, forced into the unenviable role of 'companion' to the pitiless old woman. An encounter with Hermann, a young German officer, in the Imperial Russian Army and an associate of her relation Tomski, seems to offer hope of escape; but it turns out Hermann has an agenda of his own.

Alexander Pushkin

– *from* The Queen of Spades (1834) –

Hermann was the son of a German settled in Russia, from whom he had inherited a small sum of money. Firmly resolved to preserve his independence, he had made it a principle not to touch his private income. He lived on his pay, and did not allow himself the slightest luxury. He was not very communicative; and his reserve rendered it difficult for his comrades to amuse themselves at his expense.

Under an assumed calm he concealed strong passions and a highly-imaginative disposition. But he was always master of himself, and kept himself free from the ordinary faults of young men. Thus, a gambler by temperament, he never touched a card, feeling, as he himself said, that his position did not allow him to 'risk the necessary in view of the superfluous.' Yet he would pass entire nights before a card table, watching with feverish anxiety the rapid changes of the game. The anecdote of Count Saint-Germaine's three cards* had struck his imagination, and he did nothing but think of it all that night.

* It is believed that the Count has initiated the Countess into a magical secret: three cards which, if played in the correct order, will infallibly win the game.

'If,' he said to himself next day as he was walking along the streets of St. Petersburg, 'if she would only tell me her secret – if she would only name the three winning cards! I must get presented to her, that I may pay my court and gain her confidence. Yes! And she is eighty-seven! She may die this week – tomorrow perhaps. But after all, is there a word of truth in the story? No! Economy, Temperance, Work; these are my three winning cards. With them I can double my capital; increase it tenfold. They alone can ensure my independence and prosperity.'

Dreaming in this way as he walked along, his attention was attracted by a house built in an antiquated style of architecture. The street was full of carriages, which passed one by one before the old house, now brilliantly illuminated. As the people stepped out of the carriages Hermann saw now the little feet of a young woman, now the military boot of a general. Then came a clocked stocking; then, again, a diplomatic pump. Fur-lined cloaks and coats passed in procession before a gigantic porter.

Hermann stopped. 'Who lives here?' he said to a watchman in his box.

'The Countess Anna Fedotovna.' It was Tomski's grandmother.

Hermann started. The story of the three cards came once more upon his imagination. He walked to and fro before the house, thinking of the woman to whom it belonged, of her wealth and her mysterious power. At last he returned to his den. But for some time he could not get to sleep; and when at last sleep came upon him, he saw, dancing before his eyes, cards, a green table, and heaps of rubles and banknotes. He saw himself doubling stake after stake, always winning, and then filling his pockets with piles of coin, and stuffing his pocketbook with countless banknotes. When he awoke, he sighed to find that his treasures were but creations of a disordered fancy; and, to drive such thoughts from him, he went out for a walk. But he had not gone far when he found himself once more before the house of the Countess. He seemed to have been attracted there by some irresistible force. He stopped, and looked up at the windows. There he saw a girl's head with beautiful black hair, leaning gracefully over a book or an embroidery-frame. The head was lifted, and he saw a fresh complexion and black eyes.

This moment decided his fate.

Some days afterwards, a young person with lively eyes called to see Miss Lisaveta, on the part of a milliner. Lisaveta wondered what she could want, and suspected, as she received her, some secret intention. She was much surprised, however, when she recognised, on the letter that was now handed to her, the writing of Hermann.

'You make a mistake,' she said; 'this letter is not for me.'

'I beg your pardon,' said the milliner, with a slight

smile; 'be kind enough to read it.'

Lisaveta glanced at it. Hermann was asking for an appointment.

'Impossible!' she cried, alarmed both at the boldness of the request, and at the manner in which it was made. 'This letter is not for me,' she repeated; and she tore it into a hundred pieces.

'If the letter was not for you, why did you tear it up? You should have given it me back, that I might take it to the person it was meant for.'

'True,' said Lisaveta, quite disconcerted. 'But bring me no more letters, and tell the person who gave you this one that he ought to blush for his conduct.'

Hermann, however, was not a man to give up what he had once undertaken. Every day Lisaveta received a fresh letter from him, sent now in one way, now in another. They were no longer translated from the German. Hermann wrote under the influence of a commanding passion, and spoke a language which was his own. Lisaveta could not hold out against such torrents of eloquence. She received the letters, kept them, and at last answered them. Every day her answers were longer and more affectionate, until at last she threw out of the window a letter couched as follows:

This evening there is a ball at the Embassy. The Countess will be there. We shall remain until two in the morning. You may manage to see me alone. As soon as the Countess leaves home, that is to say towards eleven o'clock, the servants are sure to go out, and there will be no one left but the porter, who will be sure to be asleep in his box. Enter as soon as it strikes eleven, and go upstairs as fast as possible. If you find anyone in the antechamber, ask whether the Countess is at home, and you will be told that she is out, and, in that case, you must resign yourself, and go away. In all probability, however, you will meet no one. The Countess's women are together in a distant room. When you are once in the antechamber, turn to the left, and walk straight on, until you reach the Countess's bedroom. There, behind a large screen, you will see two doors. The one on the right leads to a dark room. The one on the left leads to a corridor, at the end of which is a little winding staircase, which leads to my parlour.

At, ten o'clock Hermann was already on duty before the Countess's door. It was a frightful night. The winds had been unloosed, and the snow was falling in large flakes; the lamps gave an uncertain light; the streets were deserted; from time to time passed a sledge, drawn by a wretched hack, on the lookout for a fare. Covered by a thick overcoat, Hermann felt neither the wind nor the snow. At last the Countess's carriage drew up. He saw two huge footmen come forward and take beneath the arms a dilapidated spectre, and place it on the cushions well wrapped up in an enormous fur cloak. Immediately afterwards, in a cloak of lighter make, her head crowned with natural flowers, came Lisaveta, who sprang into the carriage like a dart. The door was closed, and the carriage rolled on softly over the snow.

The porter closed the street door, and soon the windows of the first floor became dark. Silence reigned throughout the house. Hermann walked backwards and forwards; then coming to a lamp he looked at his watch. It was twenty minutes to eleven. Leaning against the lamp-post, his eyes fixed on the long hand of his watch, he counted impatiently the minutes which had yet to pass. At eleven o'clock precisely Hermann walked up the steps, pushed open the street door, and went into the vestibule, which was well lighted. As it happened the porter was not there. With a firm and rapid step he rushed up the staircase and reached the antechamber. There, before a lamp, a footman was sleeping, stretched out in a dirty greasy dressing gown. Hermann passed quickly before him and crossed the dining-room and the drawing-room, where there was no light. But the lamp of the antechamber helped him to see. At last he reached the Countess's bedroom. Before a screen covered with old icons (sacred pictures) a golden lamp was burning. Gilt armchairs, sofas of faded colours, furnished with soft cushions, were arranged symmetrically along the walls, which were hung with China silk. He saw two large portraits painted by Madame le Brun. One represented a man of forty, stout and full coloured, dressed in a light green coat, with a decoration on his breast. The second portrait was that of an elegant young woman, with an aquiline nose, powdered hair rolled back on the temples, and with a rose over her ear. Everywhere might be seen shepherds and shepherdesses in Dresden china, with vases of all shapes, clocks by Leroy, work baskets, fans, and all the thousand playthings for the use of ladies of fashion, discovered in the last century, at the time of Montgolfier's balloons and Mesmer's animal magnetism.

Hermann passed behind the screen, which concealed a little iron bedstead. He saw the two doors; the one on the right leading to the dark room, the one on the left to the corridor. He opened the latter, saw the staircase which led to the poor little companion's parlour, and then, closing this door, went into the dark room.

The time passed slowly. Everything was quiet in the house. The drawing-room clock struck midnight, and again there was silence. Hermann was standing up, leaning against the stove, in which there was no fire. He was calm; but his heart beat with quick pulsations, like that of a man determined to brave all dangers he might have to meet, because he knows them to be inevitable. He heard one o'clock strike; then two; and soon afterwards the distant roll of a carriage. He now, in spite of himself, experienced some emotion. The carriage approached rapidly and stopped. There was at once a great noise of servants running about the staircases, and a confusion of voices. Suddenly the rooms were all lit up, and the Countess's three antiquated maids came at once into the bedroom. At last appeared the Countess herself.

The walking mummy sank into a large Voltaire armchair. Hermann looked through the crack in the door; he saw Lisaveta pass close to him, and heard her hurried step as she went up the little winding staircase. For a moment he felt something like remorse; but it soon passed off, and his heart was once more of stone.

The Countess began to undress before a looking-glass. Her headdress of roses was taken off, and her powdered wig separated from her own hair, which was very short and quite white. Pins fell in showers around her. At last she was in her dressing gown and night cap, and in this costume, more suitable to her age, was less hideous than before.

Like most old people, the Countess was tormented by sleeplessness. She had her armchair rolled towards one of the windows, and told her maids to leave her. The lights were put out, and the room was lighted only by the lamp which burned before the holy images. The Countess, sallow and wrinkled, balanced herself gently from right to left. In her dull eyes could be read an utter absence of thought; and as she moved from side to side, one might have said that she did so not by any action of the will, but through some secret mechanism.

Suddenly this death's-head assumed a new expression; the lips ceased to tremble, and the eyes became alive. A strange man had appeared before the Countess!

It was Hermann.

'Do not be alarmed, madam,' said Hermann, in a

low voice, but very distinctly. 'For the love of Heaven, do not be alarmed. I do not wish to do you the slightest harm; on the contrary, I come to implore a favour of you.'

The old woman looked at him in silence, as if she did not understand. Thinking she was deaf, he leaned towards her ear and repeated what he had said; but the Countess still remained silent.

'You can ensure the happiness of my whole life, and without it costing you a farthing. I know that you can name to me three cards –'

The Countess now understood what he required.

'It was a joke,' she interrupted. 'I swear to you it was only a joke.'

'No, madam,' replied Hermann in an angry tone. 'Remember Tchaplitzki, and how you enabled him to win.'

The Countess was agitated. For a moment her features expressed strong emotion; but they soon resumed their former dullness.

'Cannot you name to me,' said Hermann, 'three winning cards?'

The Countess remained silent. 'Why keep this secret for your great-grandchildren,' he continued. 'They are rich enough without; they do not know the value of money. Of what profit would your three cards be to them? They are debauchees. The man who cannot keep his inheritance will die in want, though he had the science of demons at his command. I am a steady man. I know the value of money. Your three cards will not be lost upon me. Come!'

He stopped tremblingly, awaiting a reply. The Countess did not utter a word. Hermann went upon his knees.

'If your heart has ever known the passion of love; if you can remember its sweet ecstasies; if you have ever been touched by the cry of a newborn babe; if any human feeling has ever caused your heart to beat, I entreat you by the love of a husband, a lover, a mother, by all that is sacred in life, not to reject my prayer. Tell me your secret! Reflect! You are old; you have not long to live! Remember that the happiness of a man is in your hands; that not only myself, but my children and my grandchildren will bless your memory as a saint.'

The old Countess answered not a word.

Hermann rose, and drew a pistol from his pocket.

'Hag!' he exclaimed, 'I will make you speak.'

At the sight of the pistol the Countess for the second time showed agitation. Her head shook violently and she stretched out her hands as if to put the weapon aside. Then suddenly she fell back motionless.

'Come, don't be childish!' said Hermann. 'I adjure you for the last time; will you name the three cards?'

The Countess did not answer. Hermann saw that she was dead!

[. . .]

✟ Partly for form's sake, partly out of superstitious dread, Hermann presents himself at the Countess's funeral where, according to Russian Orthodox tradition, her body is on display in an open coffin. But as he joins the others in paying their respects, he is horrified to see her dead face wink at him mockingly. Thoroughly shocked by the experience, Hermann resorts to a tried and tested Russian remedy.

In a quiet restaurant, where he took his meals, he, contrary to his habit, drank a great deal of wine, with the object of stupefying himself. But the wine had no effect but to excite his imagination, and give fresh activity to the ideas with which he was preoccupied.

He went home earlier than usual, lay down with his clothes on upon the bed, and fell into a leaden sleep. When he woke up it was night, and the room was lighted up by the rays of the moon. He looked at his watch; it was a quarter to three. He could sleep no more. He sat up on the bed and thought of the old Countess. At this moment someone in the street passed the window, looked into the room, and then went on. Hermann scarcely noticed it; but in another minute he heard the door of the antechamber open. He thought that his orderly, drunk as usual, was returning from some nocturnal excursion; but the step was one to which he was not accustomed. Somebody seemed to be softly walking over the floor in slippers.

The door opened, and a woman, dressed entirely in white, entered the bedroom. Hermann thought it

33

must be his old nurse, and he asked himself what she could want at that time of night.

But the woman in white, crossing the room with a rapid step, was now at the foot of his bed, and Hermann recognised the Countess.

'I come to you against my wish,' she said in a firm voice. 'I am forced to grant your prayer. Three, seven, ace, will win, if played one after the other; but you must not play more than one card in twenty-four hours, and afterwards, as long as you live, you must never touch a card again. I forgive you my death on condition of your marrying my companion, Lisaveta Ivanovna.'

With these words she walked towards the door, and gliding with her slippers over the floor, disappeared. Hermann heard the door of the antechamber open, and soon afterwards saw a white figure pass along the street. It stopped for a moment before his window, as if to look at him.

Hermann remained, for some time astounded. Then he got up and went into the next room. His orderly, drunk as usual, was asleep on the floor. He had much difficulty in waking him, and then could not obtain from him the least explanation. The door of the antechamber was locked.

[. . .]

✝ Thoroughly obsessed by the dead Countess's revelation, Hermann decides that it's time to put the magic formula to the test. (Her 'condition' regarding Lisaveta has evidently been forgotten.) Hermann's friend Narumoff takes him to the house of the notorious gambler Tchekalinski, who welcomes him with warm, but at the same time faintly carnivorous courtesy.

Tchekalinski took him by the hand, told him that he was glad to see him, that no one stood on ceremony in his house; and then went on dealing. The deal occupied some time, and stakes were made on more than thirty cards. Tchekalinski waited patiently to allow the winners time to double their stakes, paid what he had lost, listened politely to all observations, and, more politely still, put straight the corners of cards, when in a fit of absence someone had taken the liberty of turning them down. At last when the game was at an end, Tchekalinski collected the cards, shuffled them again, had them cut, and then dealt anew.

'Will you allow me to take a card?' said Hermann, stretching out his arm above a fat man who occupied nearly the whole of one side of the table. Tchekalinski, with a gracious smile, bowed in consent. Naroumoff complimented Hermann, with a laugh, on the cessation of the austerity by which his conduct had hitherto been marked, and wished him all kinds of happiness on the occasion of his first appearance in the character of a gambler.

'There!' said Hermann, after writing some figures on the back of his card.

'How much?' asked the banker, half closing his

eyes. 'Excuse me, I cannot see.'

'Forty-seven thousand rubles,' said Hermann.

Everyone's eyes were directed towards the new player.

'He has lost his head,' thought Naroumoff.

'Allow me to point out to you,' said Tchekalinski, with his eternal smile, 'that you are playing rather high. We never put down here, as a first stake, more than a hundred and seventy-five rubles.'

'Very well,' said Hermann, 'but do you accept my stake or not?'

Tchekalinski bowed in token of acceptation. 'I only wish to point out to you,' he said, 'that although I am perfectly sure of my friends, I can only play against ready money. I am quite convinced that your word is as good as gold; but to keep up the rules of the game, and to facilitate calculations, I should be obliged to you if you would put the money on your card.'

Hermann took a banknote from his pocket and handed it to Tchekalinski, who, after examining it with a glance, placed it on Hermann's card.

Then he began to deal. He turned up on the right a ten, and on the left a three.

'I win,' said Hermann, exhibiting his three.

A murmur of astonishment ran through the assembly. The banker knitted his eyebrows, but speedily his face resumed its everlasting smile.

'Shall I settle at once?' he asked.

'If you will be kind enough to do so,' said Hermann.

Tchekalinski took a bundle of banknotes from his pocketbook, and paid. Hermann pocketed his winnings and left the table.

Narumoff was lost in astonishment. Hermann drank a glass of lemonade and went home.

The next evening he returned to the house. Tchekalinski again held the bank. Hermann went to the table, and this time the players hastened to make room for him. Tchekalinski received him with a most gracious bow. Hermann waited, took a card, and staked on it his forty-seven thousand roubles, together with the like sum which he had gained the evening before.

Tchekalinski began to deal. He turned up on the right a knave, and on the left a seven.

Hermann exhibited a seven.

There was a general exclamation. Tchekalinski was evidently ill at ease, but he counted out the ninety-four thousand roubles to Hermann, who took them in the calmest manner, rose from the table, and went away.

The next evening, at the accustomed hour, he again appeared. Everyone was expecting him. Generals and high officials had left their whist to watch this extraordinary play. The young officers had quitted their sofas, and even the servants of the house pressed round the table.

When Hermann took his seat, the other players ceased to stake, so impatient were they to see him have it out with the banker, who, still smiling, watched the approach of his antagonist and prepared to meet him. Each of them untied at the same time a pack of cards. Tchekalinski shuffled, and Hermann cut. Then the latter took up a card and covered it with a heap of banknotes. It was like the preliminaries of a duel. A deep silence reigned through the room.

Tchekalinski took up the cards with trembling hands and dealt. On one side he put down a queen and on the other side an ace.

'Ace wins,' said Hermann.

'No. Queen loses,' said Tchekalinski.

Hermann looked. Instead of ace, he saw a queen of spades before him. He could not trust his eyes! And now as he gazed, in fascination, on the fatal card, he fancied that he saw the queen of spades open and then close her eye, while at the same time she gave a mocking smile. He felt a thrill of nameless horror. The queen of spades resembled the dead Countess!

Hermann is now at the Obukhoff Asylum, room No. 17 a hopeless madman! He answers no questions which we put to him. Only he mumbles to himself without cessation, 'Three, seven, ace; three, seven, *queen*!'

From *The Queen of Spades*, translated from the Russian by Mrs. Sutherland Edwards,1892

✟ Another account of the lasting impact of a supernatural encounter occurs in the famous ghost story 'Oh, Whistle, and I'll Come to You, My Lad' by the Edwardian scholar and antiquary M. R. James. The title comes from an eerie, intensely erotic poem by Robert Burns, in which a young woman promises to answer her suitor's whistle-call, 'Tho' father an' mother an' a' should gae mad . . .' What that might mean for the hero of James's story is, to some extent, left for the reader to guess. If the introductory section seems a little unpromising – the kind of donnish banter one might expect of an old-world Oxbridge common room where women are scarcely mentioned, let alone entertained – that only makes what follows all the more, well, extraordinary. Slowly, by deftly engineered degrees, James takes us into a world way beyond the imaginings of his hapless 'Professor of Ontography'.

M. R. James

– *from* 'Oh, Whistle, and I'll Come to You, My Lad' (1904) –

'I suppose you will be getting away pretty soon, now Full term is over, Professor,' said a person not in the story to the Professor of Ontography, soon after they had sat down next to each other at a feast in the hospitable hall of St. James's College.

The Professor was young, neat, and precise in speech.

'Yes,' he said; 'my friends have been making me take up golf this term, and I mean to go to the East Coast – in point of fact to Burnstow – (I dare say you know it) for a week or ten days, to improve my game. I hope to get off tomorrow.'

'Oh, Parkins,' said his neighbour on the other side, 'if you are going to Burnstow, I wish you would look at the site of the Templars' preceptory, and let me know if you think it would be any good to have a dig there in the summer.'

It was, as you might suppose, a person of antiquarian pursuits who said this, but, since he merely appears in this prologue, there is no need to give his entitlements.

'Certainly,' said Parkins, the Professor: 'if you will describe to me whereabouts the site is, I will do my best to give you an idea of the lie of the land when I get back; or I could write to you about it, if you would tell me where you are likely to be.'

'Don't trouble to do that, thanks. It's only that I'm thinking of taking my family in that direction in the Long, and it occurred to me that, as very few of the English preceptories have ever been properly planned, I might have an opportunity of doing something useful on off-days.'

The Professor rather sniffed at the idea that planning out a preceptory could be described as useful. His neighbour continued:

'The site – I doubt if there is anything showing above ground – must be down quite close to the beach now. The sea has encroached tremendously, as you know, all along that bit of coast. I should think, from the map, that it must be about three-quarters of a mile from the Globe Inn, at the north end of the town. Where are you going to stay?'

'Well, *at* the Globe Inn, as a matter of fact,' said Parkins; 'I have engaged a room there. I couldn't get in anywhere else; most of the lodging-houses are shut up in winter, it seems; and, as it is, they tell me that the only room of any size I can have is really a double-bedded one, and that they haven't a corner in which to store the other bed, and so on. But I must have a fairly large room, for I am taking some books down, and mean to do a bit of work; and though I don't quite fancy having an empty bed – not to speak of two – in what I may call for the time being my study, I suppose I can manage to rough it for the short time I shall be there.'

'Do you call having an extra bed in your room roughing it, Parkins?' said a bluff person opposite. 'Look here, I shall come down and occupy it for a bit; it'll be company for you.'

The Professor quivered, but managed to laugh in a courteous manner.

'By all means, Rogers; there's nothing I should like better. But I'm afraid you would find it rather dull; you don't play golf, do you?'

'No, thank Heaven!' said rude Mr. Rogers.

'Well, you see, when I'm not writing I shall most likely be out on the links, and that, as I say, would be rather dull for you, I'm afraid.'

'Oh, I don't know! There's certain to be somebody I know in the place; but, of course, if you don't want me, speak the word, Parkins; I shan't be offended. Truth, as you always tell us, is never offensive.'

Parkins was, indeed, scrupulously polite and strictly truthful. It is to be feared that Mr. Rogers sometimes practised upon his knowledge of these characteristics. In Parkins's breast there was a conflict now raging, which for a moment or two did not allow him to answer. That interval being over, he said:

'Well, if you want the exact truth, Rogers, I was considering whether the room I speak of would really be large enough to accommodate us both comfortably;

and also whether (mind, I shouldn't have said this if you hadn't pressed me) you would not constitute something in the nature of a hindrance to my work.'

Rogers laughed loudly.

'Well done, Parkins!' he said. 'It's all right. I promise not to interrupt your work; don't you disturb yourself about that. No, I won't come if you don't want me; but I thought I should do so nicely to keep the ghosts off.' Here he might have been seen to wink and to nudge his next neighbour. Parkins might also have been seen to become pink. 'I beg pardon, Parkins,' Rogers continued; 'I oughtn't to have said that. I forgot you didn't like levity on these topics.'

'Well,' Parkins said, 'as you have mentioned the matter, I freely own that I do *not* like careless talk about what you call ghosts. A man in my position,' he went on, raising his voice a little, 'cannot, I find, be too careful about appearing to sanction the current beliefs on such subjects. As you know, Rogers, or as you ought to know; for I think I have never concealed my views – '

'No, you certainly have not, old man,' put in Rogers *sotto voce*.

'– I hold that any semblance, any appearance of concession to the view that such things might exist is equivalent to a renunciation of all that I hold most sacred. But I'm afraid I have not succeeded in securing your attention.'

'Your *undivided* attention, was what Dr. Blimber

actually *said*,'* Rogers interrupted, with every appearance of an earnest desire for accuracy. 'But I beg your
pardon, Parkins: I'm stopping you.'

'No, not at all,' said Parkins. 'I don't remember
Blimber; perhaps he was before my time. But I needn't
go on. I'm sure you know what I mean.'

'Yes, yes,' said Rogers, rather hastily – 'just so.
We'll go into it fully at Burnstow, or somewhere.'

In repeating the above dialogue I have tried to give
the impression which it made on me, that Parkins was
something of an old woman – rather hen-like, perhaps,
in his little ways; totally destitute, alas! of the sense of
humour, but at the same time dauntless and sincere in
his convictions, and a man deserving of the greatest
respect. Whether or not the reader has gathered so
much, that was the character which Parkins had.

On the following day Parkins did, as he had hoped,
succeed in getting away from his college, and in arriving
at Burnstow. He was made welcome at the Globe Inn,
was safely installed in the large double-bedded room
of which we have heard, and was able before retiring
to rest to arrange his materials for work in apple-pie
order upon a commodious table which occupied the
outer end of the room, and was surrounded on three
sides by windows looking out seaward; that is to say,
the central window looked straight out to sea, and

* Mr. Rogers was wrong, *vide Dombey and Son*, chapter xii. [James's
note]

those on the left and right commanded prospects along the shore to the north and south respectively. On the south you saw the village of Burnstow. On the north no houses were to be seen, but only the beach and the low cliff backing it. Immediately in front was a strip – not considerable – of rough grass, dotted with old anchors, capstans, and so forth; then a broad path; then the beach. Whatever may have been the original distance between the Globe Inn and the sea, not more than sixty yards now separated them.

The rest of the population of the inn was, of course, a golfing one, and included few elements that call for a special description. The most conspicuous figure was, perhaps, that of an *ancient militaire*, secretary of a London club, and possessed of a voice of incredible strength, and of views of a pronouncedly Protestant type. These were apt to find utterance after his attendance upon the ministrations of the Vicar, an estimable man with inclinations towards a picturesque ritual, which he gallantly kept down as far as he could out of deference to East Anglian tradition.

Professor Parkins, one of whose principal characteristics was pluck, spent the greater part of the day following his arrival at Burnstow in what he had called improving his game, in company with this Colonel Wilson; and during the afternoon – whether the process of improvement were to blame or not, I am not sure – the Colonel's demeanour assumed a colouring so lurid that even Parkins jibbed at the thought of walking home with him from the links. He determined, after a short and furtive look at that bristling moustache and those incarnadined features, that it would be wiser to allow the influences of tea and tobacco to do what they could with the Colonel before the dinner-hour should render a meeting inevitable.

'I might walk home tonight along the beach,' he reflected – 'yes, and take a look – there will be light enough for that – at the ruins of which Disney was talking. I don't exactly know where they are, by the way; but I expect I can hardly help stumbling on them.'

This he accomplished, I may say, in the most literal sense, for in picking his way from the links to the shingle beach his foot caught, partly in a gorse root and partly in a biggish stone, and over he went. When he got up and surveyed his surroundings, he found himself in a patch of somewhat broken ground covered with small depressions and mounds. These latter, when he came to examine them, proved to be simply masses of flints embedded in mortar and grown over with turf. He must, he quite rightly concluded, be on the site of the preceptory he had promised to look at. It seemed not unlikely to reward the spade of the explorer; enough of the foundations was probably left at no great depth to throw a good deal of light on the general plan. He remembered vaguely that the Templars, to whom this site had belonged, were in the habit of building round churches, and he thought a particular series of the humps or mounds near him did appear to be arranged in something of a circular form. Few people can resist the temptation to try a little amateur research in a department quite outside their own, if only for the satisfaction of showing how successful they would have been had they only taken it up seriously. Our Professor, however, if he felt something of this mean desire, was also truly anxious to oblige Mr. Disney. So he paced with care the circular area he had noticed, and wrote down its rough dimensions in his pocket-book. Then he proceeded to examine an oblong eminence which lay east of the centre of the circle, and seemed to his thinking likely to be the base of a platform or altar. At one end of it, the northern, a patch of the turf was gone – removed by some boy or other creature *ferae naturae*. It might, he thought, be as well to probe the soil here for evidences of masonry, and he took out his knife and began scraping away the earth. And now followed another little discovery: a portion of soil fell inward as he scraped, and disclosed a small cavity. He lighted one match after another to help him to see of what nature the hole was, but the wind was too strong for them all. By tapping and scratching the sides with his knife, however, he was able to make out that it must be an artificial hole in masonry. It was rectangular, and the sides, top, and bottom, if not actually plastered, were smooth and regular. Of course it was empty. No! As he withdrew the knife he heard a metallic clink, and when he introduced his hand it met with a cylindrical object lying on the floor of the hole. Naturally enough, he picked it up, and when he brought it into the light, now fast fading, he could see that it, too, was of man's making – a metal tube about four inches long, and evidently of some considerable age.

By the time Parkins had made sure that there was nothing else in this odd receptacle, it was too late and too dark for him to think of undertaking any further search. What he had done had proved so unexpectedly interesting that he determined to sacrifice a little more of the daylight on the morrow to archaeology. The object which he now had safe in his pocket was bound to be of some slight value at least, he felt sure.

Bleak and solemn was the view on which he took a last look before starting homeward. A faint yellow light in the west showed the links, on which a few figures moving towards the clubhouse were still visible, the squat Martello tower, the lights of Aldsey village, the pale ribbon of sands intersected at intervals by black wooden groynes, the dim and murmuring sea. The wind was bitter from the north, but was at his back when he set out for the Globe. He quickly rattled and clashed through the shingle and gained the sand, upon which, but for the groynes which had to be got over every few yards, the going was both good and quiet. One last look behind, to measure the distance he had made since leaving the ruined Templars' church, showed him a prospect of company on his walk, in the shape of a rather indistinct personage, who seemed to be making great efforts to catch up with him, but made little, if any, progress. I mean that there was an appearance of running about his movements, but that the distance between him and Parkins did not seem materially to lessen. So, at least, Parkins thought, and decided that he almost certainly did not know him, and that it would be absurd to wait until he came up. For all that, company, he began to think, would really be very welcome on that lonely shore, if only you could choose your companion. In his unenlightened days he had read of meetings in such places which even now would hardly bear thinking of. He went on thinking of them, however, until he reached home, and particularly of one which catches most people's fancy at some time of their childhood. 'Now I saw in my dream that Christian had gone but a very little way when he saw a foul fiend coming over the field to meet him.' 'What should I do now,' he thought, 'if I looked back and caught sight of a black figure sharply defined against the yellow sky, and saw that it had horns and wings? I wonder whether I should stand or run for it. Luckily, the gentleman behind is not of that kind, and he seems to be about as far off now as when I saw him first. Well, at this rate he won't get his dinner as soon as I shall; and, dear me! it's within a quarter of an hour of the time now. I must run!'

Parkins had, in fact, very little time for dressing. When he met the Colonel at dinner, Peace – or as much of her as that gentleman could manage – reigned once more in the military bosom; nor was she put to flight in the hours of bridge that followed dinner, for Parkins was a more than respectable player. When, therefore, he retired towards twelve o'clock, he felt that he had spent his evening in quite a satisfactory way, and that, even for so long as a fortnight or three weeks, life at the Globe would be supportable under similar conditions – 'especially,' thought he, 'if I go on improving my game.'

As he went along the passages he met the boots of the Globe, who stopped and said:

'Beg your pardon, sir, but as I was a-brushing your coat just now there was somethink fell out of the pocket. I put it on your chest of drawers, sir, in your room, sir – a piece of a pipe or somethink of that, sir. Thank you, sir. You'll find it on your chest of drawers, sir – yes, sir. Good night, sir.'

The speech served to remind Parkins of his little discovery of that afternoon. It was with some considerable curiosity that he turned it over by the light of his candles. It was of bronze, he now saw, and was shaped very much after the manner of the modern dog-whistle; in fact it was – yes, certainly it was – actually no more nor less than a whistle. He put it to his lips, but it was quite full of a fine, caked-up sand or earth, which would not yield to knocking, but must be loosened with a knife. Tidy as ever in his habits, Parkins cleared out the earth on to a piece of paper, and took the latter to the window to empty it out. The night was clear and bright, as he saw when he had opened the casement, and he stopped for an instant to look at the sea and note a belated wanderer stationed on the shore in front of the inn. Then he shut the window, a little surprised at the late hours people kept at Burnstow, and took his whistle to the light again. Why, surely there were marks on it, and not merely marks, but letters! A very little rubbing rendered the deeply-cut inscription quite legible, but the Professor had to confess, after some earnest thought, that the meaning of it was as obscure to him as the writing on the wall to Belshazzar. There were legends both on the front and on the back of the whistle. The one read thus:

FLA

FUR BIS

FLE

The other:

卐 QUIS EST ISTE QUI UENIT 卐

'I ought to be able to make it out,' he thought; 'but I suppose I am a little rusty in my Latin. When I come to think of it, I don't believe I even know the word for a whistle. The long one does seem simple enough. It ought to mean, "Who is this who is coming?" Well, the best way to find out is evidently to whistle for him.'

He blew tentatively and stopped suddenly, startled and yet pleased at the note he had elicited. It had a quality of infinite distance in it, and, soft as it was, he somehow felt it must be audible for miles round. It was a sound, too, that seemed to have the power (which many scents possess) of forming pictures in the brain. He saw quite clearly for a moment a vision of a wide, dark expanse at night, with a fresh wind blowing, and in the midst a lonely figure – how employed, he could not tell. Perhaps he would have seen more had not the picture been broken by the sudden surge of a gust of wind against his casement, so sudden that it made him look up, just in time to see the white glint of a sea-bird's wing somewhere outside the dark panes.

The sound of the whistle had so fascinated him that he could not help trying it once more, this time more boldly. The note was little, if at all, louder than before, and repetition broke the illusion – no picture followed, as he had half hoped it might. 'But what is this? Goodness! what force the wind can get up in a few minutes! What a tremendous gust! There! I knew that window-fastening was no use! Ah! I thought so – both candles out. It's enough to tear the room to pieces.'

The first thing was to get the window shut. While you might count twenty Parkins was struggling with the small casement, and felt almost as if he were pushing back a sturdy burglar, so strong was the pressure. It slackened all at once, and the window banged to and latched itself. Now to relight the candles and see what damage, if any, had been done. No, nothing seemed amiss; no glass even was broken in the casement. But the noise had evidently roused at least one member of the household: the Colonel was to be heard stumping in his stockinged feet on the floor above, and growling.

Quickly as it had risen, the wind did not fall at once. On it went, moaning and rushing past the house, at times rising to a cry so desolate that, as Parkins disinterestedly said, it might have made fanciful people feel quite uncomfortable; even the unimaginative, he thought after a quarter of an hour, might be happier without it.

Whether it was the wind, or the excitement of golf, or of the researches in the preceptory that kept Parkins awake, he was not sure. Awake he remained, in any case, long enough to fancy (as I am afraid I often do myself under such conditions) that he was the victim of all manner of fatal disorders: he would lie counting the beats of his heart, convinced that it was going to stop work every moment, and would entertain grave suspicions of his lungs, brain, liver, etc. – suspicions which he was sure would be dispelled by the return of daylight, but which until then refused to be put aside. He found a little vicarious comfort in the idea that someone else was in the same boat. A near neighbour (in the darkness it was not easy to tell his direction) was tossing and rustling in his bed, too.

The next stage was that Parkins shut his eyes and determined to give sleep every chance. Here again over-excitement asserted itself in another form – that of making pictures. *Experto crede*, pictures do come to the closed eyes of one trying to sleep, and are often so little to his taste that he must open his eyes and disperse them.

Parkins's experience on this occasion was a very distressing one. He found that the picture which presented itself to him was continuous. When he opened his eyes, of course, it went; but when he shut them once more it framed itself afresh, and acted itself out again, neither quicker nor slower than before. What he saw was this:

A long stretch of shore – shingle edged by sand, and intersected at short intervals with black groynes running down to the water – a scene, in fact, so like that of his afternoon's walk that, in the absence of any landmark, it could not be distinguished therefrom. The light was obscure, conveying an impression of gathering storm, late winter evening, and slight cold rain. On this bleak stage at first no actor was visible. Then, in the distance, a bobbing black object appeared; a moment more, and it was a man running, jumping, clambering over the groynes, and every few seconds looking eagerly back. The nearer he came the more obvious it was that he was not only anxious, but even terribly frightened, though his face was not to be distinguished. He was, moreover, almost at the end of his strength. On he came; each successive obstacle seemed to cause him more difficulty than the last. 'Will he get over this next one?' thought Parkins; 'it seems a little higher than the others.' Yes; half climbing, half throwing himself, he did get over, and fell all in a heap on the other side (the side nearest to the spectator). There, as if really unable to get up again, he remained crouching under the groyne, looking up in an attitude of painful anxiety.

So far no cause whatever for the fear of the runner had been shown; but now there began to be seen, far up the shore, a little flicker of something light-coloured moving to and fro with great swiftness and irregularity. Rapidly growing larger, it, too, declared itself as a figure in pale, fluttering draperies, ill-defined. There was something about its motion which made Parkins very unwilling to see it at close quarters. It would stop, raise arms, bow itself towards the sand, then run stooping across the beach to the water-edge and back again; and then, rising upright, once more continue its course forward at a speed that was startling and terrifying. The moment came when the pursuer was hovering about from left to right only a few yards beyond the groyne where the runner lay in hiding. After two or three ineffectual castings hither and thither it came to a stop, stood upright, with arms raised high, and then darted straight forward towards the groyne.

It was at this point that Parkins always failed in his resolution to keep his eyes shut. With many misgivings as to incipient failure of eyesight, over-worked brain, excessive smoking, and so on, he finally resigned himself to light his candle, get out a book, and pass the night waking, rather than be tormented by this persistent panorama, which he saw clearly enough could only be a morbid reflection of his walk and his thoughts on that very day.

The scraping of match on box and the glare of light must have startled some creatures of the night – rats or what not – which he heard scurry across the floor from the side of his bed with much rustling. Dear, dear! the match is out! Fool that it is! But the second one burnt better, and a candle and book were duly procured, over which Parkins pored till sleep of a wholesome kind came upon him, and that in no long space. For about the first time in his orderly and prudent life he forgot to blow out the candle, and when he was called next morning at eight there was still a flicker in the socket and a sad mess of guttered grease on the top of the little table.

After breakfast he was in his room, putting the finishing touches to his golfing costume – fortune had again allotted the Colonel to him for a partner – when one of the maids came in.

'Oh, if you please,' she said, 'would you like any extra blankets on your bed, sir?'

'Ah! thank you,' said Parkins. 'Yes, I think I should like one. It seems likely to turn rather colder.'

In a very short time the maid was back with the blanket.

'Which bed should I put it on, sir?' she asked.

'What? Why, that one – the one I slept in last night,' he said, pointing to it.

'Oh yes! I beg your pardon, sir, but you seemed to have tried both of 'em; leastways, we had to make 'em both up this morning.'

'Really? How very absurd!' said Parkins. 'I certainly never touched the other, except to lay some things on it. Did it actually seem to have been slept in?'

'Oh yes, sir!' said the maid. 'Why, all the things was crumpled and throwed about all ways, if you'll excuse me, sir – quite as if anyone 'adn't passed but a very poor night, sir.'

'Dear me,' said Parkins. 'Well, I may have disordered it more than I thought when I unpacked my things. I'm very sorry to have given you the extra trouble, I'm sure. I expect a friend of mine soon, by the way – a gentleman from Cambridge – to come and occupy it for a night or two. That will be all right, I suppose, won't it?'

'Oh yes, to be sure, sir. Thank you, sir. It's no trouble, I'm sure,' said the maid, and departed to giggle with her colleagues.

Parkins set forth, with a stern determination to improve his game.

I am glad to be able to report that he succeeded so far in this enterprise that the Colonel, who had been rather repining at the prospect of a second day's play in his company, became quite chatty as the morning advanced; and his voice boomed out over the flats, as certain also of our own minor poets have said, 'like some great bourdon in a minster tower.'

'Extraordinary wind, that, we had last night,' he said. 'In my old home we should have said someone had been whistling for it.'

'Should you, indeed!' said Parkins. 'Is there a superstition of that kind still current in your part of the country?'

'I don't know about superstition,' said the Colonel. 'They believe in it all over Denmark and Norway, as well as on the Yorkshire coast; and my experience is, mind you, that there's generally something at the bottom of what these country-folk hold to, and have held to for generations. But it's your drive' (or whatever it might have been: the golfing reader will have to imagine appropriate digressions at the proper intervals).

When conversation was resumed, Parkins said, with a slight hesitancy:

'Apropos of what you were saying just now, Colonel, I think I ought to tell you that my own views on such subjects are very strong. I am, in fact, a convinced disbeliever in what is called the "supernatural."'

'What!' said the Colonel, 'do you mean to tell me you don't believe in second-sight, or ghosts, or anything of that kind?'

'In nothing whatever of that kind,' returned Parkins firmly.

'Well,' said the Colonel, 'but it appears to me at that rate, sir, that you must be little better than a Sadducee.'

Parkins was on the point of answering that, in his opinion, the Sadducees were the most sensible persons he had ever read of in the Old Testament; but, feeling some doubt as to whether much mention of them was to be found in that work, he preferred to laugh the accusation off.

'Perhaps I am,' he said; 'but – Here, give me my cleek, boy! – Excuse me one moment, Colonel.' A short interval. 'Now, as to whistling for the wind, let me give you my theory about it. The laws which govern winds are really not at all perfectly known – to fisher-folk and such, of course, not known at all. A man or woman of eccentric habits, perhaps, or a stranger, is seen repeatedly on the beach at some unusual hour, and is heard whistling. Soon afterwards a violent wind rises; a man who could read the sky perfectly or who possessed a barometer could have foretold that it would. The simple people of a fishing-village have no barometers, and only a few rough rules for prophesying weather. What more natural than that the eccentric personage I postulated should be regarded as having raised the wind, or that he or she should clutch eagerly at the reputation of being able to do so? Now, take last night's wind: as it happens, I myself was whistling. I blew a whistle twice, and the wind seemed to come absolutely in answer to my call. If anyone had seen me – '

The audience had been a little restive under this harangue, and Parkins had, I fear, fallen somewhat into the tone of a lecturer; but at the last sentence the Colonel stopped.

'Whistling, were you?' he said. 'And what sort of whistle did you use? Play this stroke first.' Interval.

'About that whistle you were asking, Colonel. It's rather a curious one. I have it in my – No; I see I've left it in my room. As a matter of fact, I found it yesterday.'

And then Parkins narrated the manner of his discovery of the whistle, upon hearing which the Colonel grunted, and opined that, in Parkins's place, he should himself be careful about using a thing that had belonged to a set of Papists, of whom, speaking generally, it might be affirmed that you never knew what they might not have been up to. From this topic he diverged to the enormities of the Vicar, who had given notice on the previous Sunday that Friday would be the Feast of St. Thomas the Apostle, and that there would be service at eleven o'clock in the church. This and other similar proceedings constituted in the Colonel's view a strong presumption that the Vicar was a concealed Papist, if not a Jesuit; and Parkins, who could not very readily follow the Colonel in this region, did not disagree with him. In fact, they got on so well together in the morning that there was no talk on either side of their separating after lunch.

Both continued to play well during the afternoon, or, at least, well enough to make them forget everything else until the light began to fail them. Not until then did Parkins remember that he had meant to do some more investigating at the preceptory; but it was of no great importance, he reflected. One day was as good as another; he might as well go home with the Colonel.

As they turned the corner of the house, the Colonel was almost knocked down by a boy who rushed into him at the very top of his speed, and then, instead of running away, remained hanging on to him and panting. The first words of the warrior were naturally those of reproof and objurgation, but he very quickly discerned that the boy was almost speechless with fright. Inquiries were useless at first. When the boy got his breath he began to howl, and still clung to the Colonel's legs. He was at last detached, but continued to howl.

'What in the world *is* the matter with you? What have you been up to? What have you seen?' said the two men.

'Ow, I seen it wive at me out of the winder,' wailed the boy, 'and I don't like it.'

'What window?' said the irritated Colonel. 'Come, pull yourself together, my boy.'

'The front winder it was, at the 'otel,' said the boy.

At this point Parkins was in favour of sending the boy home, but the Colonel refused; he wanted to get to the bottom of it, he said; it was most dangerous to give a boy such a fright as this one had had, and if it turned out that people had been playing jokes, they should suffer for it in some way. And by a series of questions he made out this story: the boy had been playing about on the grass in front of the Globe with some others; then they had gone home to their teas, and he was just going, when he happened to look up at the front winder and see it a-wiving at him. *It* seemed to be a figure of some sort, in white as far as he knew – couldn't see its face; but it wived at him, and it warn't a right thing – not to say not a right person. Was there a light in the room? No, he didn't think to look if there was a light. Which was the window? Was it the top one or the second one? The seckind one it was – the big winder what got two little uns at the sides.

'Very well, my boy,' said the Colonel, after a few more questions. 'You run away home now. I expect it was some person trying to give you a start. Another time, like a brave English boy, you just throw a stone – well, no, not that exactly, but you go and speak to the waiter, or to Mr. Simpson, the landlord, and – yes – and say that I advised you to do so.'

The boy's face expressed some of the doubt he felt as to the likelihood of Mr. Simpson's lending a favourable ear to his complaint, but the Colonel did not appear to perceive this, and went on:

'And here's a sixpence – no, I see it's a shilling – and you be off home, and don't think any more about it.'

The youth hurried off with agitated thanks, and the Colonel and Parkins went round to the front of the Globe and reconnoitred. There was only one window answering to the description they had been hearing.

'Well, that's curious,' said Parkins; 'it's evidently my window the lad was talking about. Will you come up for a moment, Colonel Wilson? We ought to be able to see if anyone has been taking liberties in my room.'

They were soon in the passage, and Parkins made as if to open the door. Then he stopped and felt in his pockets.

'This is more serious than I thought,' was his next remark. 'I remember now that before I started this morning I locked the door. It is locked now, and, what is more, here is the key.' And he held it up. 'Now,' he went on, 'if the servants are in the habit of going into one's room during the day when one is away, I can only say that – well, that I don't approve of it at all.' Conscious of a somewhat weak climax, he busied himself in opening the door (which was indeed locked) and in lighting candles. 'No,' he said, 'nothing seems disturbed.'

'Except your bed,' put in the Colonel.

'Excuse me, that isn't my bed,' said Parkins. 'I don't use that one. But it does look as if someone had been playing tricks with it.'

It certainly did: the clothes were bundled up and twisted together in a most tortuous confusion. Parkins pondered.

'That must be it,' he said at last: 'I disordered the clothes last night in unpacking, and they haven't made it since. Perhaps they came in to make it, and that boy saw them through the window; and then they were

64

called away and locked the door after them. Yes, I think that must be it.'

'Well, ring and ask,' said the Colonel, and this appealed to Parkins as practical.

The maid appeared, and, to make a long story short, deposed that she had made the bed in the morning when the gentleman was in the room, and hadn't been there since. No, she hadn't no other key. Mr. Simpson he kep' the keys; he'd be able to tell the gentleman if anyone had been up.

This was a puzzle. Investigation showed that nothing of value had been taken, and Parkins remembered the disposition of the small objects on tables and so forth well enough to be pretty sure that no pranks had been played with them. Mr. and Mrs. Simpson furthermore agreed that neither of them had given the duplicate key of the room to any person whatever during the day. Nor could Parkins, fair-minded man as he was, detect anything in the demeanour of master, mistress, or maid that indicated guilt. He was much more inclined to think that the boy had been imposing on the Colonel.

The latter was unwontedly silent and pensive at dinner and throughout the evening. When he bade good night to Parkins, he murmured in a gruff undertone:

'You know where I am if you want me during the night.'

'Why, yes, thank you, Colonel Wilson, I think I

do; but there isn't much prospect of my disturbing you, I hope. By the way,' he added, 'did I show you that old whistle I spoke of? I think not. Well, here it is.'

The Colonel turned it over gingerly in the light of the candle.

'Can you make anything of the inscription?' asked Parkins, as he took it back.

'No, not in this light. What do you mean to do with it?'

'Oh, well, when I get back to Cambridge I shall submit it to some of the archaeologists there, and see what they think of it; and very likely, if they consider it worth having, I may present it to one of the museums.'

"M!' said the Colonel. 'Well, you may be right. All I know is that, if it were mine, I should chuck it straight into the sea. It's no use talking, I'm well aware, but I expect that with you it's a case of live and learn. I hope so, I'm sure, and I wish you a good night.'

He turned away, leaving Parkins in act to speak at the bottom of the stair, and soon each was in his own bedroom.

By some unfortunate accident, there were neither blinds nor curtains to the windows of the Professor's room. The previous night he had thought little of this, but tonight there seemed every prospect of a bright moon rising to shine directly on his bed, and probably wake him later on. When he noticed this he was a good deal annoyed, but, with an ingenuity which I can only envy, he succeeded in rigging up, with the help of a railway rug, some safety pins, and a stick and umbrella, a screen which, if it only held together, would completely keep the moonlight off his bed. And shortly afterwards he was comfortably in that bed. When he had read a somewhat solid work long enough to produce a decided wish for sleep, he cast a drowsy glance round the room, blew out the candle, and fell back upon the pillow.

He must have slept soundly for an hour or more, when a sudden clatter shook him up in a most unwelcome manner. In a moment he realized what had happened: his carefully constructed screen had given way, and a very bright frosty moon was shining directly on his face. This was highly annoying. Could he possibly get up and reconstruct the screen? or could he manage to sleep if he did not?

For some minutes he lay and pondered over the possibilities; then he turned over sharply, and with all his eyes open lay breathlessly listening. There had been a movement, he was sure, in the empty bed on the opposite side of the room. Tomorrow he would have it moved, for there must be rats or something playing about in it. It was quiet now. No! the commotion began again. There was a rustling and shaking: surely more than any rat could cause.

I can figure to myself something of the Professor's bewilderment and horror, for I have in a dream thirty years back seen the same thing happen; but the reader will hardly, perhaps, imagine how dreadful it was to him to see a figure suddenly sit up in what he had known was an empty bed. He was out of his own bed in one bound, and made a dash towards the window, where lay his only weapon, the stick with which he had propped his screen. This was, as it turned out, the worst thing he could have done, because the personage in the empty bed, with a sudden smooth motion, slipped from the bed and took up a position, with outspread arms, between the two beds, and in front of the door. Parkins watched it in a horrid perplexity. Somehow, the idea of getting past it and escaping through the door was intolerable to him; he could not have borne – he didn't know why – to touch it; and as for its touching him, he would sooner dash himself through the window than have that happen. It stood for the moment in a band of dark shadow, and he had not seen what its face was like. Now it began to move, in a stooping posture, and all at once the spectator realized, with some horror and some relief, that it must be blind, for it seemed to feel about it with its muffled arms in a groping and random fashion. Turning half away from him, it became suddenly conscious of the bed he had just left, and darted towards it, and bent over and felt the pillows in a way which made Parkins shudder as he had never in his life thought it possible. In a very few moments it seemed to know that the bed was empty, and then, moving forward into the area of light and facing the window, it showed for the first time what manner of thing it was.

Parkins, who very much dislikes being questioned about it, did once describe something of it in my hearing, and I gathered that what he chiefly remembers about it is a horrible, an intensely horrible, face *of crumpled linen*. What expression he read upon it he could not or would not tell, but that the fear of it went nigh to maddening him is certain.

But he was not at leisure to watch it for long. With formidable quickness it moved into the middle of the room, and, as it groped and waved, one corner of its draperies swept across Parkins's face. He could not – though he knew how perilous a sound was – he could not keep back a cry of disgust, and this gave the searcher an instant clue. It leapt towards him upon the instant, and the next moment he was halfway through the window backwards, uttering cry upon cry at the utmost pitch of his voice, and the linen face was thrust close into his own. At this, almost the last possible second, deliverance came, as you will have guessed: the Colonel burst the door open, and was just in time to see the dreadful group at the window. When he reached the figures only one was left. Parkins sank forward into the room in a faint, and before him on the floor lay a tumbled heap of bedclothes.

Colonel Wilson asked no questions, but busied himself in keeping everyone else out of the room and in getting Parkins back to his bed; and himself, wrapped in a rug, occupied the other bed for the rest of the night. Early on the next day Rogers arrived, more welcome than he would have been a day before, and the three of them held a very long consultation in the Professor's room. At the end of it the Colonel left the hotel door carrying a small object between his finger and thumb, which he cast as far into the sea as a very brawny arm could send it. Later on the smoke of a burning ascended from the back premises of the Globe.

Exactly what explanation was patched up for the staff and visitors at the hotel I must confess I do not recollect. The Professor was somehow cleared of the ready suspicion of *delirium tremens*, and the hotel of the reputation of a troubled house.

There is not much question as to what would have happened to Parkins if the Colonel had not intervened when he did. He would either have fallen out of the window or else lost his wits. But it is not so evident what more the creature that came in answer to the whistle could have done than frighten. There seemed to be absolutely nothing material about it save the bed-clothes of which it had made itself a body. The Colonel, who remembered a not very dissimilar occurrence in India, was of opinion that if Parkins had closed with it, it could really have done very little, and that its one power was that of frightening. The whole thing, he said, served to confirm his opinion of the Church of Rome.

There is really nothing more to tell, but, as you may imagine, the Professor's views on certain points are less clear cut than they used to be. His nerves, too, have suffered: he cannot even now see a surplice hanging on a door quite unmoved, and the spectacle of a scarecrow in a field late on a winter afternoon has cost him more than one sleepless night.

From *Ghost Stories of an Antiquary*, 1904

✝ It isn't difficult to identify the point at which Professor Parkins takes his fatal turning: quite simply, having taken that whistle, he should never have blown it. At the same time, however, the story hints delicately that there's more to this sense of 'wrongness' than initially meets the reader's eye. Remember the discovery of the whistle in the ruins of a Templars' preceptory: such structures, as James informs us almost casually, were circular; and, in magical rites, circles are traditionally regarded as safe spaces, protecting the magician or witch from the elemental powers he or she summons. But Parkins blows the whistle in his hotel bedroom, which – it's safe to infer – is as rational and rectangular as Parkin's logical, rigidly unimaginative mind. If so, it offers no protection against the anarchic, irrational, alarmingly intimate force he unwittingly unleashes.

✝ There is no suggestion in 'Oh, Whistle, and I'll Come to You, My Lad' that the 'creature' that came in answer to Professor Parkins's unwitting summons is, or ever was, in any way human, which is one of the reasons that climactic image of the 'face of crumpled linen' is so disturbing. Is it better or worse, though, when the face is, or at least could be, that of an identifiable human being? Caution is necessary here, because so much in Henry James's masterpiece *The Turn of the Screw* can be read in more than one way, especially the motivations of the central character, the governess sent to tutor two mysteriously parentless, 'preternaturally' charming children at their remote East Anglian home. Her account of why she accepted the bizarre posting in the first place (the first of many possible wrong turnings), from a 'guardian' who apparently wants nothing to do with the children at all, is more striking for what it conceals than what it reveals. Even in this one short chapter there are so many points at which one would like to assume the role of psychoanalyst, or possibly detective, and stop her with some such formulation as, 'Now, what precisely do you mean by . . . ?' As for the encounter itself, having read it once, why not go back and reread the first section, the governess's patently rose-tinted account of her sessions with her 'innocent' young charges – wilfully rose-tinted, one might conclude, in view of the fact that something, either in the house or in the children themselves, has evidently spooked her? Who is deluding whom here, and in what way might that be the factor that summons the figure on the stairs?

Henry James

– *from* The Turn of the Screw (1898) –

I waited and waited, and the days, as they elapsed, took something from my consternation. A very few of them, in fact, passing, in constant sight of my pupils, without a fresh incident, sufficed to give to grievous fancies and even to odious memories a kind of brush of the sponge. I have spoken of the surrender to their extraordinary childish grace as a thing I could actively cultivate, and it may be imagined if I neglected now to address myself to this source for whatever it would yield. Stranger than I can express, certainly, was the effort to struggle against my new lights; it would doubtless have been, however, a greater tension still had it not been so frequently successful. I used to wonder how my little charges could help guessing that I thought strange things about them; and the circumstances that these things only made them more interesting was not by itself a direct aid to keeping them in the dark. I trembled lest they should see that they were so immensely more interesting. Putting things at the worst, at all events, as in meditation I so often did, any clouding of their innocence could only be – blameless and foredoomed as they were – a reason the more for taking risks. There were moments when, by an irresistible impulse, I found myself catching them up and pressing them to my heart. As soon as I had done so I used to say to myself: 'What will they think of that? Doesn't it betray too much?' It would have been easy to get into a sad, wild tangle about how much I might betray; but the real account, I feel, of the hours of peace that I could still enjoy was that the immediate charm of my companions was a beguilement still effective even under the shadow of the possibility that it was studied. For if it occurred to me that I might occasionally excite suspicion by the little outbreaks of my sharper passion for them, so too I remember wondering if I mightn't see a queerness in the traceable increase of their own demonstrations.

They were at this period extravagantly and preternaturally fond of me; which, after all, I could reflect, was no more than a graceful response in children perpetually bowed over and hugged. The homage of which they were so lavish succeeded, in truth, for my nerves, quite as well as if I never appeared to myself, as I may say, literally to catch them at a purpose in it. They had never, I think, wanted to do so many things for their poor protectress; I mean – though they got their lessons better and better, which was naturally what would please her most – in the way of diverting, entertaining, surprising her; reading her passages, telling her stories, acting her charades, pouncing out at her, in disguises, as animals and historical characters, and above all astonishing her by the 'pieces' they had secretly got by heart and could interminably recite. I should never get to the bottom – were I to let myself go even now – of the prodigious private commentary, all under still more private correction, with which, in these days, I overscored their full hours. They had shown me from the first a facility for everything, a general faculty which, taking a fresh start, achieved remarkable flights. They got their little tasks as if they loved them, and indulged, from the mere exuberance of the gift, in the most unimposed little miracles of memory. They not only popped out at me as tigers and as Romans, but as Shakespeareans, astronomers, and navigators. This was so singularly the case that it had presumably much to do with the fact as to which, at the present day, I am at a loss for a different explanation: I allude to my unnatural composure on the subject of another school for Miles. What I remember is that I was content not, for the time, to open the question, and that contentment must have sprung from the sense of his perpetually striking show of cleverness. He was too clever for a bad governess, for a parson's daughter, to spoil; and the strangest if not the brightest thread in the pensive embroidery I just spoke of was the impression I might have got, if I had dared to work it out, that he was under some influence operating in his small intellectual life as a tremendous incitement.

If it was easy to reflect, however, that such a boy could postpone school, it was at least as marked that for such a boy to have been 'kicked out' by a schoolmaster was a mystification without end. Let me add that in their company now – and I was careful almost never to be out of it – I could follow no scent very far. We lived in a cloud of music and love and success and private theatricals. The musical sense in each of the children was of the quickest, but the elder in especial had a marvelous knack of catching and repeating. The schoolroom piano broke into all gruesome fancies; and when that failed there were confabulations in corners, with a sequel of one of them going out in the highest spirits in order to 'come in' as something new. I had had brothers myself, and it was no revelation to me that little girls could be slavish idolaters of little boys. What surpassed everything was that there was a little boy in the world who could have for the inferior age, sex, and intelligence so fine a consideration. They were extraordinarily at one, and to say that they never either quarreled or complained is to make the note of praise coarse for their quality of sweetness. Sometimes, indeed, when I dropped into coarseness, I perhaps came across traces of little understandings between them by which one of them should keep me occupied while the other slipped away. There is a *naïf* side, I suppose, in all diplomacy; but if my pupils practiced upon me, it was surely with the minimum of grossness. It was all in the other quarter that, after a lull, the grossness broke out.

I find that I really hang back; but I must take my plunge. In going on with the record of what was hideous at Bly, I not only challenge the most liberal faith – for which I little care; but – and this is another matter – I renew what I myself suffered, I again push my way through it to the end. There came suddenly an hour after which, as I look back, the affair seems to me to have been all pure suffering; but I have at least reached the heart of it, and the straightest road out is doubtless to advance. One evening – with nothing to lead up or to prepare it – I felt the cold touch of the impression that had breathed on me the night of my arrival and which, much lighter then, as I have mentioned, I should probably have made little of in memory had my subsequent sojourn been less agitated. I had not gone to bed; I sat reading by a couple of candles. There was a roomful of old books at Bly – last-century fiction, some of it, which, to the extent of a distinctly deprecated renown, but never to so much as that of a stray specimen, had reached the sequestered home and appealed to the unavowed curiosity of my youth. I remember that the book I had in my hand was Fielding's *Amelia*; also that I was wholly awake. I recall further both a general conviction that it was horribly late and a particular objection to looking at my watch. I figure, finally, that the white curtain draping, in the fashion of those days, the head of Flora's little bed, shrouded, as I had assured myself long before, the perfection of childish rest. I recollect in short that, though I was deeply interested in my author, I found myself, at the turn of a page and with his spell all scattered, looking straight up from him and hard at the door of my room. There was a moment during which I listened, reminded of the faint sense I had had, the first night, of there being something undefinably astir in the house, and noted the soft breath of the open casement just move the half-drawn blind. Then, with all the marks of a deliberation that must have seemed magnificent had there been anyone to admire it, I laid down my book, rose to my feet, and, taking a candle, went straight out of the room and, from the passage, on which my light made little impression, noiselessly closed and locked the door.

I can say now neither what determined nor what guided me, but I went straight along the lobby, holding my candle high, till I came within sight of the tall window that presided over the great turn of the staircase. At this point I precipitately found myself aware of three things. They were practically simultaneous, yet they had flashes of succession. My candle, under a bold flourish, went out, and I perceived, by the uncovered window, that the yielding dusk of earliest morning rendered it unnecessary. Without it, the next instant, I saw that there was someone on the stair. I speak of sequences, but I required no lapse of seconds to stiffen myself for a third encounter with Quint. The apparition had reached the landing halfway up and was therefore on the spot nearest the window, where at sight of me, it stopped short and fixed me exactly as it had fixed me from the tower and from the garden. He knew me as well as I knew him; and so, in the cold, faint twilight, with a glimmer in the high glass and another on the polish of the oak stair below, we faced each other in our common intensity. He was absolutely, on this occasion, a living, detestable, dangerous presence. But that was not the wonder of wonders; I reserve this distinction for quite another circumstance: the circumstance that dread had unmistakably quitted me and that there was nothing in me there that didn't meet and measure him.

I had plenty of anguish after that extraordinary moment, but I had, thank God, no terror. And he knew I had not – I found myself at the end of an instant magnificently aware of this. I felt, in a fierce rigor of confidence, that if I stood my ground a minute I should cease – for the time, at least – to have him to reckon with; and during the minute, accordingly, the thing was as human and hideous as a real interview: hideous just because it *was* human, as human as to have met alone, in the small hours, in a sleeping house, some enemy, some adventurer, some criminal. It was the dead silence of our long gaze at such close quarters that gave the whole horror, huge as it was, its only note of the unnatural. If I had met a murderer in such a place and at such an hour, we still at least would have spoken. Something would have passed, in life, between us; if nothing had passed, one of us would have moved. The moment was so prolonged that it would have taken but little more to make me doubt if even *I* were in life. I can't express what followed it save by saying that the silence itself – which was indeed in a manner an attestation of my strength – became the element into which I saw the figure disappear; in which I definitely saw it turn as I might have seen the low wretch to which it had once belonged turn on receipt of an order, and pass, with my eyes on the villainous back that no hunch could have more disfigured, straight down the staircase and into the darkness in which the next bend was lost.

✝ Draw up a list of the most enduringly popular Victorian and Edwardian ghost stories and it's striking how many of them are either by women, or by men of ambivalent sexuality – both Henry and M. R. James very much a case in point. There's something about the medium that makes it particularly apt for coded or oblique expressions of 'the love that dare not speak its name'. For women writers especially it could be a highly effective channel for the embodiment and discharge of repressed emotions: sexual impulses perhaps, or related creative forces, so much harder for women to express in a society unwilling to accept that women even had the potential for such dangerous energies.

There may also be an element of revenge: Freud's 'return of the repressed' as the goddess Nemesis, intent on punishing the cold male rationality that would deny even her existence. Charlotte Perkins Gilman's *The Yellow Wallpaper*, published six years before *The Turn of the Screw*, has a strong claim to be considered the first great feminist ghost story. As soon as we learn that husband John 'has no patience with faith, an intense horror of superstition, and he scoffs openly at any talk of things not to be felt and seen and put down in figures', we know he's as good as lost the battle already. But what does happen exactly? Is there a ghost? And who exactly is speaking in those chilling final sentences? If we persist in asking those kinds of questions, the story seems to warn, then we're making the same fatal mistake as 'that man'.

Charlotte Perkins Gilman

– The Yellow Wallpaper (1892) –

It is very seldom that mere ordinary people like John and myself secure ancestral halls for the summer.

A colonial mansion, a hereditary estate, I would say a haunted house, and reach the height of romantic felicity – but that would be asking too much of fate!

Still I will proudly declare that there is something queer about it.

Else, why should it be let so cheaply? And why have stood so long untenanted?

John laughs at me, of course, but one expects that in marriage.

John is practical in the extreme. He has no patience with faith, an intense horror of superstition, and he scoffs openly at any talk of things not to be felt and seen and put down in figures.

John is a physician, and *perhaps* – (I would not say it to a living soul, of course, but this is dead paper and a great relief to my mind) – *perhaps* that is one reason I do not get well faster.

You see, he does not believe I am sick!

And what can one do?

If a physician of high standing, and one's own

husband, assures friends and relatives that there is really nothing the matter with one but temporary nervous depression – a slight hysterical tendency – what is one to do?

My brother is also a physician, and also of high standing, and he says the same thing.

So I take phosphates or phosphites – whichever it is, and tonics, and journeys, and air, and exercise, and am absolutely forbidden to 'work' until I am well again.

Personally, I disagree with their ideas.

Personally, I believe that congenial work, with excitement and change, would do me good.

But what is one to do?

I did write for a while in spite of them; but it *does* exhaust me a good deal – having to be so sly about it, or else meet with heavy opposition.

I sometimes fancy that in my condition if I had less opposition and more society and stimulus – but John says the very worst thing I can do is to think about my condition, and I confess it always makes me feel bad.

So I will let it alone and talk about the house.

The most beautiful place! It is quite alone, standing well back from the road, quite three miles from the village. It makes me think of English places that you read about, for there are hedges and walls and gates that lock, and lots of separate little houses for the gardeners and people.

There is a *delicious* garden! I never saw such a garden – large and shady, full of box-bordered paths, and lined with long grape-covered arbors with seats under them.

There were greenhouses, too, but they are all broken now.

There was some legal trouble, I believe, something about the heirs and co-heirs; anyhow, the place has been empty for years.

That spoils my ghostliness, I am afraid; but I don't care – there is something strange about the house – I can feel it.

I even said so to John one moonlight evening, but he said what I felt was a *draught*, and shut the window.

I get unreasonably angry with John sometimes. I'm sure I never used to be so sensitive. I think it is due to this nervous condition.

But John says if I feel so I shall neglect proper self-control; so I take pains to control myself – before him, at least, and that makes me very tired.

I don't like our room a bit. I wanted one downstairs that opened on the piazza and had roses all over the window, and such pretty old-fashioned chintz hangings! but John would not hear of it.

He said there was only one window and not room for two beds, and no near room for him if he took another.

He is very careful and loving, and hardly lets me stir without special direction.

I have a schedule prescription for each hour in the day; he takes all care from me, and so I feel basely ungrateful not to value it more.

He said we came here solely on my account, that I was to have perfect rest and all the air I could get. 'Your exercise depends on your strength, my dear,' said he, 'and your food somewhat on your appetite; but air you can absorb all the time.' So we took the nursery, at the top of the house.

It is a big, airy room, the whole floor nearly, with windows that look all ways, and air and sunshine galore. It was a nursery first and then playground and gymnasium, I should judge; for the windows are barred for little children, and there are rings and things in the walls.

The paint and paper look as if a boys' school had used it. It is stripped off – the paper – in great patches all around the head of my bed, about as far as I can reach, and in a great place on the other side of the room low down. I never saw a worse paper in my life.

One of those sprawling flamboyant patterns committing every artistic sin.

It is dull enough to confuse the eye in following, pronounced enough to constantly irritate, and provoke study, and when you follow the lame, uncertain curves for a little distance they suddenly commit suicide – plunge off at outrageous angles, destroy themselves in unheard-of contradictions.

The color is repellant,[*] almost revolting; a

---

* Arsenic had been used as a colouring in wallpaper since the late eighteenth century. Its harmful effects – on the mind as well as the body – were already known by the time Gilman wrote this story.

smouldering, unclean yellow, strangely faded by the slow-turning sunlight.

It is a dull yet lurid orange in some places, a sickly sulphur tint in others.

No wonder the children hated it! I should hate it myself if I had to live in this room long.

There comes John, and I must put this away, – he hates to have me write a word.

We have been here two weeks, and I haven't felt like writing before, since that first day.

I am sitting by the window now, up in this atrocious nursery, and there is nothing to hinder my writing as much as I please, save lack of strength.

John is away all day, and even some nights when his cases are serious.

I am glad my case is not serious!

But these nervous troubles are dreadfully depressing.

John does not know how much I really suffer. He knows there is no *reason* to suffer, and that satisfies him.

Of course it is only nervousness. It does weigh on me so not to do my duty in any way!

I meant to be such a help to John, such a real rest and comfort, and here I am a comparative burden already!

Nobody would believe what an effort it is to do what little I am able – to dress and entertain, and order things.

It is fortunate Mary is so good with the baby. Such a dear baby!

And yet I *cannot* be with him, it makes me so nervous.

I suppose John never was nervous in his life. He laughs at me so about this wallpaper!

At first he meant to repaper the room, but afterwards he said that I was letting it get the better of me, and that nothing was worse for a nervous patient than to give way to such fancies.

He said that after the wallpaper was changed it would be the heavy bedstead, and then the barred windows, and then that gate at the head of the stairs, and so on.

'You know the place is doing you good,' he said, 'and really, dear, I don't care to renovate the house just for a three months' rental.'

'Then do let us go downstairs,' I said, 'there are such pretty rooms there.'

Then he took me in his arms and called me a blessed little goose, and said he would go down to the cellar if I wished, and have it whitewashed into the bargain.

But he is right enough about the beds and windows and things.

It is as airy and comfortable a room as any one need wish, and, of course, I would not be so silly as to make him uncomfortable just for a whim.

I'm really getting quite fond of the big room, all but that horrid paper.

Out of one window I can see the garden, those mysterious deep-shaded arbors, the riotous old-fashioned flowers, and bushes and gnarly trees.

Out of another I get a lovely view of the bay and a little private wharf belonging to the estate. There is a beautiful shaded lane that runs down there from the house. I always fancy I see people walking in these numerous paths and arbors, but John has cautioned me not to give way to fancy in the least. He says that with my imaginative power and habit of story-making a nervous weakness like mine is sure to lead to all manner of excited fancies, and that I ought to use my will and good sense to check the tendency. So I try.

I think sometimes that if I were only well enough to write a little it would relieve the press of ideas and rest me.

But I find I get pretty tired when I try.

It is so discouraging not to have any advice and companionship about my work. When I get really well John says we will ask Cousin Henry and Julia down for a long visit; but he says he would as soon put fireworks in my pillowcase as to let me have those stimulating people about now.

I wish I could get well faster.

But I must not think about that. This paper looks to me as if it *knew* what a vicious influence it had!

There is a recurrent spot where the pattern lolls like a broken neck and two bulbous eyes stare at you upside down.

I get positively angry with the impertinence of it and the everlastingness. Up and down and sideways they crawl, and those absurd, unblinking eyes are everywhere. There is one place where two breadths didn't match, and the eyes go all up and down the line, one a little higher than the other.

I never saw so much expression in an inanimate thing before, and we all know how much expression they have! I used to lie awake as a child and get more entertainment and terror out of blank walls and plain furniture than most children could find in a toy store.

I remember what a kindly wink the knobs of our big old bureau used to have, and there was one chair that always seemed like a strong friend.

I used to feel that if any of the other things looked too fierce I could always hop into that chair and be safe.

The furniture in this room is no worse than inharmonious, however, for we had to bring it all from downstairs. I suppose when this was used as a playroom they had to take the nursery things out, and no wonder! I never saw such ravages as the children have made here.

The wallpaper, as I said before, is torn off in spots, and it sticketh closer than a brother – they must have had perseverance as well as hatred.

Then the floor is scratched and gouged and splintered, the plaster itself is dug out here and there, and this great heavy bed, which is all we found in the room, looks as if it had been through the wars.

But I don't mind it a bit – only the paper.

There comes John's sister. Such a dear girl as she is, and so careful of me! I must not let her find me writing.

She is a perfect, and enthusiastic housekeeper, and hopes for no better profession. I verily believe she thinks it is the writing which made me sick!

But I can write when she is out, and see her a long way off from these windows.

There is one that commands the road, a lovely, shaded, winding road, and one that just looks off over the country. A lovely country, too, full of great elms and velvet meadows.

This wallpaper has a kind of sub-pattern in a different shade, a particularly irritating one, for you can only see it in certain lights, and not clearly then.

But in the places where it isn't faded, and where the sun is just so, I can see a strange, provoking, formless sort of figure, that seems to sulk about behind that silly and conspicuous front design.

There's sister on the stairs!

Well, the Fourth of July is over! The people are gone and I am tired out. John thought it might do me good to see a little company, so we just had mother and Nellie and the children down for a week.

Of course I didn't do a thing. Jennie sees to everything now.

But it tired me all the same.

John says if I don't pick up faster he shall send me

to Weir Mitchell in the fall.

But I don't want to go there at all. I had a friend who was in his hands once, and she says he is just like John and my brother, only more so!

Besides, it is such an undertaking to go so far.

I don't feel as if it was worthwhile to turn my hand over for anything, and I'm getting dreadfully fretful and querulous.

I cry at nothing, and cry most of the time.

Of course I don't when John is here, or anybody else, but when I am alone.

And I am alone a good deal just now. John is kept in town very often by serious cases, and Jennie is good and lets me alone when I want her to.

So I walk a little in the garden or down that lovely lane, sit on the porch under the roses, and lie down up here a good deal.

I'm getting really fond of the room in spite of the wallpaper. Perhaps *because* of the wallpaper.

It dwells in my mind so!

I lie here on this great immovable bed – it is nailed down, I believe – and follow that pattern about by the hour. It is as good as gymnastics, I assure you. I start, we'll say, at the bottom, down in the corner over there where it has not been touched, and I determine for the thousandth time that I *will* follow that pointless pattern to some sort of a conclusion.

I know a little of the principle of design, and I know this thing was not arranged on any laws of radiation, or alternation, or repetition, or symmetry, or anything else that I ever heard of.

It is repeated, of course, by the breadths, but not otherwise.

Looked at in one way each breadth stands alone, the bloated curves and flourishes – a kind of 'debased Romanesque' with *delirium tremens* – go waddling up and down in isolated columns of fatuity.

But, on the other hand, they connect diagonally, and the sprawling outlines run off in great slanting waves of optic horror, like a lot of wallowing seaweeds in full chase.

The whole thing goes horizontally, too, at least it seems so, and I exhaust myself in trying to distinguish the order of its going in that direction.

They have used a horizontal breadth for a frieze, and that adds wonderfully to the confusion.

There is one end of the room where it is almost intact, and there, when the cross-lights fade and the low sun shines directly upon it, I can almost fancy radiation after all, – the interminable grotesques seem to form around a common centre and rush off in headlong plunges of equal distraction.

It makes me tired to follow it. I will take a nap, I guess.

I don't know why I should write this.

I don't want to.

I don't feel able.

And I know John would think it absurd. But I *must* say what I feel and think in some way – it is such a relief!

But the effort is getting to be greater than the relief.

Half the time now I am awfully lazy, and lie down ever so much.

John says I musn't lose my strength, and has me take cod-liver oil and lots of tonics and things, to say nothing of ale and wine and rare meat.

Dear John! He loves me very dearly, and hates to have me sick. I tried to have a real earnest reasonable talk with him the other day, and tell him how I wish he would let me go and make a visit to Cousin Henry and Julia.

But he said I wasn't able to go, nor able to stand it after I got there; and I did not make out a very good case for myself, for I was crying before I had finished.

It is getting to be a great effort for me to think straight. Just this nervous weakness, I suppose.

And dear John gathered me up in his arms, and just carried me upstairs and laid me on the bed, and sat by me and read to me till it tired my head.

He said I was his darling and his comfort and all he had, and that I must take care of myself for his sake, and keep well.

He says no one but myself can help me out of it, that I must use my will and self-control and not let any silly fancies run away with me.

There's one comfort, the baby is well and happy,

and does not have to occupy this nursery with the horrid wallpaper.

If we had not used it that blessed child would have! What a fortunate escape! Why, I wouldn't have a child of mine, an impressionable little thing, live in such a room for worlds.

I never thought of it before, but it is lucky that John kept me here after all. I can stand it so much easier than a baby, you see.

Of course I never mention it to them anymore, – I am too wise, – but I keep watch of it all the same.

There are things in that paper that nobody knows but me, or ever will.

Behind that outside pattern the dim shapes get clearer every day.

It is always the same shape, only very numerous.

And it is like a woman stooping down and creeping about behind that pattern. I don't like it a bit. I wonder – I begin to think – I wish John would take me away from here!

It is so hard to talk with John about my case, because he is so wise, and because he loves me so.

But I tried it last night.

It was moonlight. The moon shines in all around, just as the sun does.

I hate to see it sometimes, it creeps so slowly, and always comes in by one window or another.

John was asleep and I hated to waken him, so I kept

still and watched the moonlight on that undulating wallpaper till I felt creepy.

The faint figure behind seemed to shake the pattern, just as if she wanted to get out.

I got up softly and went to feel and see if the paper *did* move, and when I came back John was awake.

'What is it, little girl?' he said. 'Don't go walking about like that – you'll get cold.'

I thought it was a good time to talk, so I told him that I really was not gaining here, and that I wished he would take me away.

'Why darling!' said he, 'our lease will be up in three weeks, and I can't see how to leave before.

'The repairs are not done at home, and I cannot possibly leave town just now. Of course if you were in any danger I could and would, but you really are better, dear, whether you can see it or not. I am a doctor, dear, and I know. You are gaining flesh and color, your appetite is better. I feel really much easier about you.'

'I don't weigh a bit more,' said I, 'nor as much; and my appetite may be better in the evening, when you are here, but it is worse in the morning when you are away.'

'Bless her little heart!' said he with a big hug; 'she shall be as sick as she pleases! But now let's improve the shining hours by going to sleep, and talk about it in the morning!'

'And you won't go away?' I asked gloomily.

'Why, how can I, dear? It is only three weeks more and then we will take a nice little trip of a few days while Jennie is getting the house ready. Really, dear, you are better!'

'Better in body perhaps' – I began, and stopped short, for he sat up straight and looked at me with such a stern, reproachful look that I could not say another word.

'My darling,' said he, 'I beg of you, for my sake and for our child's sake, as well as for your own, that you will never for one instant let that idea enter your mind! There is nothing so dangerous, so fascinating, to a temperament like yours. It is a false and foolish fancy. Can you not trust me as a physician when I tell you so?'

So of course I said no more on that score, and we went to sleep before long. He thought I was asleep first, but I wasn't, and lay there for hours trying to decide whether that front pattern and the back pattern really did move together or separately.

On a pattern like this, by daylight, there is a lack of sequence, a defiance of law, that is a constant irritant to a normal mind.

The color is hideous enough, and unreliable enough, and infuriating enough, but the pattern is torturing.

You think you have mastered it, but just as you get well under way in following, it turns a back somersault and there you are. It slaps you in the face, knocks you down, and tramples upon you. It is like a bad dream.

The outside pattern is a florid arabesque, reminding one of a fungus. If you can imagine a toadstool in joints, an interminable string of toadstools, budding and sprouting in endless convolutions – why, that is something like it.

That is, sometimes!

There is one marked peculiarity about this paper, a thing nobody seems to notice but myself, and that is that it changes as the light changes.

When the sun shoots in through the east window – I always watch for that first long, straight ray – it changes so quickly that I never can quite believe it.

That is why I watch it always.

By moonlight – the moon shines in all night when there is a moon – I wouldn't know it was the same paper.

At night in any kind of light, in twilight, candlelight, lamplight, and worst of all by moonlight, it becomes bars! The outside pattern I mean, and the woman behind it is as plain as can be.

I didn't realize for a long time what the thing was that showed behind, that dim sub-pattern, but now I am quite sure it is a woman.

By daylight she is subdued, quiet. I fancy it is the pattern that keeps her so still. It is so puzzling. It keeps me quiet by the hour.

I lie down ever so much now. John says it is good for me, and to sleep all I can.

Indeed, he started the habit by making me lie down for an hour after each meal.

It is a very bad habit, I am convinced, for, you see, I don't sleep.

And that cultivates deceit, for I don't tell them I'm awake – O no!

The fact is, I am getting a little afraid of John.

He seems very queer sometimes, and even Jennie has an inexplicable look.

It strikes me occasionally, just as a scientific hypothesis, that perhaps it is the paper!

I have watched John when he did not know I was looking, and come into the room suddenly on the most innocent excuses, and I've caught him several times *looking at the paper!* And Jennie too. I caught Jennie with her hand on it once.

She didn't know I was in the room, and when I asked her in a quiet, a very quiet voice, with the most restrained manner possible, what she was doing with the paper she turned around as if she had been caught stealing, and looked quite angry – asked me why I should frighten her so!

Then she said that the paper stained everything it touched, that she had found yellow smooches on all my clothes and John's, and she wished we would be more careful!

Did not that sound innocent? But I know she was studying that pattern, and I am determined that nobody shall find it out but myself!

Life is very much more exciting now than it used to be. You see I have something more to expect, to look forward to, to watch. I really do eat better, and am more quiet than I was.

John is so pleased to see me improve! He laughed a little the other day, and said I seemed to be flourishing in spite of my wallpaper.

I turned it off with a laugh. I had no intention of telling him it was *because* of the wallpaper – he would make fun of me. He might even want to take me away.

I don't want to leave now until I have found it out. There is a week more, and I think that will be enough.

I'm feeling ever so much better! I don't sleep much at night, for it is so interesting to watch developments; but I sleep a good deal in the daytime.

In the daytime it is tiresome and perplexing.

There are always new shoots on the fungus, and new shades of yellow all over it. I cannot keep count of them, though I have tried conscientiously.

It is the strangest yellow, that wallpaper! It makes me think of all the yellow things I ever saw – not beautiful ones like buttercups, but old foul, bad yellow things.

But there is something else about that paper – the smell! I noticed it the moment we came into the room, but with so much air and sun it was not bad. Now we have had a week of fog and rain, and whether the windows are open or not, the smell is here.

It creeps all over the house.

I find it hovering in the dining-room, skulking in the parlor, hiding in the hall, lying in wait for me on the stairs.

It gets into my hair.

Even when I go to ride, if I turn my head suddenly and surprise it – there is that smell!

Such a peculiar odor, too! I have spent hours in trying to analyze it, to find what it smelled like.

It is not bad – at first, and very gentle, but quite the subtlest, most enduring odor I ever met.

In this damp weather it is awful. I wake up in the night and find it hanging over me.

It used to disturb me at first. I thought seriously of burning the house – to reach the smell.

But now I am used to it. The only thing I can think of that it is like is the *color* of the paper! A yellow smell.

There is a very funny mark on this wall, low down, near the mopboard. A streak that runs round the room. It goes behind every piece of furniture, except the bed, a long, straight, even *smooch*, as if it had been rubbed over and over.

I wonder how it was done and who did it, and what they did it for. Round and round and round – round and round and round – it makes me dizzy!

I really have discovered something at last.

Through watching so much at night, when it changes so, I have finally found out.

The front pattern *does* move – and no wonder! The woman behind shakes it!

Sometimes I think there are a great many women behind, and sometimes only one, and she crawls around fast, and her crawling shakes it all over.

Then in the very bright spots she keeps still, and in the very shady spots she just takes hold of the bars and shakes them hard.

And she is all the time trying to climb through. But nobody could climb through that pattern – it strangles so; I think that is why it has so many heads.

They get through, and then the pattern strangles them off and turns them upside down, and makes their eyes white!

If those heads were covered or taken off it would not be half so bad.

I think that woman gets out in the daytime!

And I'll tell you why – privately – I've seen her!

I can see her out of every one of my windows!

It is the same woman, I know, for she is always creeping, and most women do not creep by daylight.

I see her on that long shaded lane, creeping up and down. I see her in those dark grape arbors, creeping all around the garden.

I see her on that long road under the trees, creeping along, and when a carriage comes she hides under the blackberry vines.

I don't blame her a bit. It must be very humiliating to be caught creeping by daylight!

I always lock the door when I creep by daylight. I can't do it at night, for I know John would suspect something at once.

And John is so queer now, that I don't want to irritate him. I wish he would take another room!

Besides, I don't want anybody to get that woman out at night but myself.

I often wonder if I could see her out of all the windows at once.

But, turn as fast as I can, I can only see out of one at one time.

And though I always see her she *may* be able to creep faster than I can turn!

I have watched her sometimes away off in the open country, creeping as fast as a cloud shadow in a high wind.

If only that top pattern could be gotten off from the under one! I mean to try it, little by little.

I have found out another funny thing, but I shan't tell it this time! It does not do to trust people too much.

There are only two more days to get this paper off, and I believe John is beginning to notice. I don't like the look in his eyes.

And I heard him ask Jennie a lot of professional questions about me. She had a very good report to give.

She said I slept a good deal in the daytime.

John knows I don't sleep very well at night, for all I'm so quiet!

He asked me all sorts of questions, too, and pretended to be very loving and kind.

As if I couldn't see through him!

Still, I don't wonder he acts so, sleeping under this paper for three months.

It only interests me, but I feel sure John and Jennie are secretly affected by it.

Hurrah! This is the last day, but it is enough. John is to stay in town overnight, and won't be out until this evening.

Jennie wanted to sleep with me – the sly thing! but I told her I should undoubtedly rest better for a night all alone.

That was clever, for really I wasn't alone a bit! As soon as it was moonlight, and that poor thing began to crawl and shake the pattern, I got up and ran to help her.

I pulled and she shook, I shook and she pulled, and before morning we had peeled off yards of that paper.

A strip about as high as my head and half around the room.

And then when the sun came and that awful pattern began to laugh at me I declared I would finish it today!

We go away tomorrow, and they are moving all my furniture down again to leave things as they were before.

Jennie looked at the wall in amazement, but I told her merrily that I did it out of pure spite at the vicious thing.

She laughed and said she wouldn't mind doing it herself, but I must not get tired.

How she betrayed herself that time!

But I am here, and no person touches this paper but me – not *alive!*

She tried to get me out of the room – it was too patent! But I said it was so quiet and empty and clean now that I believed I would lie down again and sleep all I could; and not to wake me even for dinner – I would call when I woke.

So now she is gone, and the servants are gone, and the things are gone, and there is nothing left but that great bedstead nailed down, with the canvas mattress we found on it.

We shall sleep downstairs tonight, and take the boat home tomorrow.

I quite enjoy the room, now it is bare again.

How those children did tear about here!

This bedstead is fairly gnawed!

But I must get to work.

I have locked the door and thrown the key down into the front path.

I don't want to go out, and I don't want to have anybody come in, till John comes.

I want to astonish him.

I've got a rope up here that even Jennie did not find. If that woman does get out, and tries to get away, I can tie her!

But I forgot I could not reach far without anything to stand on!

This bed will *not* move!

I tried to lift and push it until I was lame, and then I got so angry I bit off a little piece at one corner – but it hurt my teeth.

Then I peeled off all the paper I could reach standing on the floor. It sticks horribly and the pattern just enjoys it! All those strangled heads and bulbous eyes and waddling fungus growths just shriek with derision!

I am getting angry enough to do something desperate. To jump out of the window would be ad- mirable exercise, but the bars are too strong even to try.

Besides I wouldn't do it. Of course not. I know well enough that a step like that is improper and might be misconstrued.

I don't like to *look* out of the windows even – there are so many of those creeping women, and they creep so fast.

I wonder if they all come out of that wallpaper as I did?

But I am securely fastened now by my well-hidden rope – you don't get *me* out in the road there!

I suppose I shall have to get back behind the pattern when it comes night, and that is hard!

It is so pleasant to be out in this great room and creep around as I please!

I don't want to go outside. I won't, even if Jennie asks me to.

For outside you have to creep on the ground, and everything is green instead of yellow.

But here I can creep smoothly on the floor, and my

shoulder just fits in that long smooch around the wall, so I cannot lose my way.

Why, there's John at the door!

It is no use, young man, you can't open it!

How he does call and pound!

Now he's crying for an axe.

It would be a shame to break down that beautiful door!

'John dear!' said I in the gentlest voice, 'the key is down by the front steps, under a plantain leaf!'

That silenced him for a few moments.

Then he said – very quietly indeed, 'Open the door, my darling!'

'I can't,' said I. 'The key is down by the front door under a plantain leaf!'

And then I said it again, several times, very gently and slowly, and said it so often that he had to go and see, and he got it, of course, and came in. He stopped short by the door.

'What is the matter?' he cried. 'For God's sake, what are you doing!'

I kept on creeping just the same, but I looked at him over my shoulder.

'I've got out at last,' said I, 'in spite of you and Jane! And I've pulled off most of the paper, so you can't put me back!'

Now why should that man have fainted? But he did, and right across my path by the wall, so that I had to creep over him every time!

✝ Nearly a hundred years after *The Yellow Wallpaper* appeared in print, Penelope Lively first published her story 'Black Dog' in the magazine *Cosmopolitan*, some of whose readers may have found their own lives – and particularly lifestyles – reflected uncomfortably in one or two of its domestic details. The situation is broadly similar to that depicted in Gilman's story, though here the reason-imagination gender polarity is rather more nuanced. The husband is another John: John Case – a highly suggestive surname, evoking not only his emblematic briefcase but also the world of the detective story, in which, conventionally, a disturbing problem is in the end reassuringly rationalised. There may even be an echo of Wittgenstein's famous assertion that 'The world is everything that is the case.' If so, then 'Black Dog' can be read as a reminder that, in the world as lived by real human beings, 'there are more things in heaven and earth . . .'

Penelope Lively

– Black Dog (1986) –

J ohn Case came home one summer evening to find
his wife huddled in the corner of the sofa with the
sitting-room curtains drawn. She said there was a black
dog in the garden, looking at her through the window.
Her husband put his briefcase in the hall and went
outside. There was no dog; a blackbird fled shriek-
ing across the lawn and next door someone was using
a mower. He did not see how any dog could get into
the garden: the fences at either side were five feet high
and there was a wall at the far end. He returned to the
house and pointed this out to his wife, who shrugged
and continued to sit hunched in the corner of the sofa.
He found her there again the next evening and at the
weekend she refused to go outside and sat for much of
the time watching the window.

The daughters came, big girls with jobs in
insurance companies, wardrobes full of bright clothes
and twenty-thousand-pound mortgages. They stood
over Brenda Case and said she should get out more.
She should go to evening classes, they said, join a
health club, do a language course, learn upholstery,
go jogging, take driving lessons. And Brenda Case sat
at the kitchen table and nodded. She quite agreed, it

would be a good thing to find a new interest – jogging, upholstery, French; yes, she said, she must pull herself together, and it was indeed up to her in the last resort, they were quite right. When they had gone she drew the sitting-room curtains again and sat on the sofa staring at a magazine they had bought. The magazine was full of recipes the daughters had said she must try; there were huge bright glossy photographs of puddings crested with Alpine peaks of cream, of dark glistening casseroles and salads like an artist's palette. The magazine costed each recipe; a four-course dinner for six worked out at £3.89 a head. It also had articles advising her on life insurance, treatment for breast cancer and how to improve her love-making.

John Case became concerned about his wife. She had always been a good housekeeper; now, they began to run out of things. When one evening there was nothing but cold meat and cheese for supper he protested. She said she had not been able to shop because it had rained all day; on rainy days the dog was always outside, waiting for her.

The daughters came again and spoke severely to their mother. They talked to their father separately, in different tones, proposing an autumn holiday in Portugal or the Canaries, a new three-piece for the sitting room, a musquash coat.

John Case discussed the whole thing with his wife, reasonably. He did this one evening after he had driven the Toyota into the garage, walked over to the front door and found it locked from within. Brenda opened it, apologized; the dog had been round at the front today, she said, sitting in the middle of the path.

He began by saying that dogs have not been known to stand on their hind legs and open doors. And in any case, he continued, there is no dog. No dog at all. The dog is something you are imagining. I have asked all the neighbours; nobody has seen a big black dog. There is no evidence of a dog. So you must stop going on about this dog because it does not exist. 'What is the matter?' he asked, gently. 'Something must be the matter. Would you like to go away on holiday? Shall we have the house redecorated?'

Brenda Case listened to him. He was sitting on the sofa, with his back to the window. She sat listening carefully to him and from time to time her eyes strayed from his face to the lawn beyond, in the middle of which the dog sat, its tongue hanging out and its yellow eyes glinting. She said she would go away for a holiday if he wished, and she would be perfectly willing for the house to be redecorated. Her husband talked about travel agents and decorating firms and once he got up and walked over to the window to inspect the condition of the paintwork; the dog, Brenda saw, continued to sit there, its eyes always on her.

They went to Marrakesh for ten days. Men came and turned the kitchen from primrose to eau-de-nil and the hallway from magnolia to parchment. September became October and Brenda Case fetched from the attic a big gnarled walking stick that was a relic of a trip to the Tyrol many years ago; she took this with her every time she went out of the house, which nowadays was not often. Inside the house, it was always somewhere near her – its end protruding from under the sofa, or hooked over the arm of her chair.

The daughters shook their tousled heads at their mother, towering over her in their baggy fashionable trousers and their big gay jackets. It's not fair on Dad, they said, can't you see that? You've only got one life, they said sternly, and Brenda Case replied that she realized that, she did indeed. Well then . . . said the daughters, one on each side of her, bigger than her, brighter, louder, always saying what they meant, going straight to the point and no nonsense, competent with income-tax returns and contemptuous of muddle.

When she was alone, Brenda Case kept doors and windows closed at all times. Occasionally, when the dog was not there, she would open the upstairs window to air the bedrooms and the bathroom; she would stand with the curtains blowing, taking in great gulps and draughts. Downstairs, of course, she would not risk this, because the dog was quite unpredictable; it would be absent all day, and then suddenly there it would be squatting by the fence, or leaning hard up against the patio doors, sprung from nowhere. She would draw the curtains, resigned, or move to another room and endure the knowledge of its presence on the other side of the wall, a few yards away. When it was there she would sit doing nothing, staring straight ahead of her; silent and patient. When it was gone she moved around the house, prepared meals, listened a little to the radio, and sometimes took the old photograph albums from the bottom drawer of the bureau in the sitting room. In these albums the daughters slowly mutated from swaddled bundles topped with monkey faces and spiky hair to chunky toddlers and then to spindly-limbed little girls in matching pinafores. They played on Cornish beaches or posed on the lawn, holding her hand (that same lawn on which the dog now sat on its hunkers). In the photographs, she looked down at them, smiling, and they gazed up at her or held out objects for her inspection – a flower, a seashell. Her husband was also in the photographs; a smaller man than now, it seemed, with a curiously vulnerable look, as though surprised in a moment of privacy. Looking at herself, Brenda saw a pretty young woman who seemed vaguely familiar, like some relative not encountered for many years.

John Case realized that nothing had been changed by Marrakesh and redecorating. He tried putting the walking stick back in the attic; his wife brought it down again. If he opened the patio doors she would simply close them as soon as he had left the room. Sometimes he saw her looking over her shoulder into the garden with an expression on her face that chilled him. He asked her, one day, what she thought the dog would do if it got into the house; she was silent for a moment and then said quietly she supposed it would eat her.

He said he could not understand, he simply did not understand, what could be wrong. It was not, he said, as though they had a thing to worry about. He gently pointed out that she wanted for nothing. It's not that we have to count the pennies any more, he said, not like in the old days.

'When we were young', said Brenda Case. 'When the girls were babies.'

'Right. It's not like that now, is it?' He indicated the 24-inch colour TV set, the video, the stereo, the microwave oven, the English Rose fitted kitchen, the bathroom with separate shower. He reminded her of the BUPA membership, the index-linked pension, the shares and dividends. Brenda agreed that it was not, it most certainly was not.

The daughters came with their boyfriends, nicely spoken confident young men in very clean shirts, who talked to Brenda of their work in firms selling computers and Japanese cameras while the girls took John into the garden and discussed their mother.

'The thing is, she's becoming agoraphobic.'

'She thinks she sees this black dog,' said John Case.

'We know,' said the eldest daughter. 'But that, frankly, is neither here nor there. It's a mechanism, simply. A ploy. Like children do. One has to get to the root of it, that's the thing.'

'It's her age,' said the youngest.

'Of course it's her age,' snorted the eldest. 'But it's

114

also her. She was always inclined to be negative, but this is ridiculous.'

'Negative?' said John Case. He tried to remember his wife – his wives – who – one of whom – he could see inside the house, beyond the glass of the patio window, looking out at him from between the two young men he hardly knew. The reflections of his daughters, his strapping prosperous daughters, were superimposed upon their mother, so that she looked at him through the cerise and orange and yellow of their clothes.

'Negative. A worrier. Look on the bright side, *I* say, but that's not Mum, is it?'

'I wouldn't have said . . .' he began.

'She's unmotivated,' said the youngest. 'That's the real trouble. No job, no nothing. It's a generation problem too.'

'I'm trying . . .' their father began.

'We know, Dad, we know. But the thing is, she needs help. This isn't something you can handle all on your own. She'll have to see someone.'

'No way', said the youngest, 'will we get Mum into therapy.'

'Dad can take her to the surgery,' said the eldest. 'For starters.'

The doctor – the new doctor, there always was a new doctor – was about the same age as her daughters, Brenda Case saw. Once upon a time doctors had been older men, fatherly and reliable. This one was good-looking, in the manner of men in knitting-pattern photographs. He sat looking at her, quite kindly, and she told him how she was feeling. In so far as this was possible.

When she had finished he tapped a pencil on his desk. 'Yes,' he said. 'Yes, I see.' And then he went on, 'There doesn't seem to be any specific trouble, does there, Mrs. Case?'

She agreed.

'How do you think you would define it yourself?'

She thought. At last she said that she supposed there was nothing wrong with her that wasn't wrong with – well, everyone.

'Quite,' said the doctor busily, writing now on his pad. 'That's the sensible way to look at things. So I'm giving you this . . . Three a day . . . Come back and see me in two weeks.'

When she had come out John Case asked to see the doctor for a moment. He explained that he was worried about his wife. The doctor nodded sympathetically. John told the doctor about the black dog, apologetically, and the doctor looked reflective for a moment and then said, 'Your wife is fifty-four.'

John Case agreed. She was indeed fifty-four.

'Exactly,' said the doctor. 'So I think we can take it that with some care and understanding these difficulties will . . . disappear. I've given her something,' he said, confidently; John Case smiled back. That was that.

'It will go away,' said John Case to his wife, firmly.

He was not entirely sure what he meant, but it did not do, he felt sure, to be irresolute. She looked at him without expression.

Brenda Case swallowed each day the pills that the doctor had given her. She believed in medicines and doctors, had always found that aspirin cured a headache and used to frequent the surgery with the girls when they were small. She was prepared for a miracle. For the first few days it seemed to her just possible that the dog was growing a little smaller but after a week she realized that it was not. She continued to take the pills and when at the end of a fortnight she told the doctor that there was no change he said that these things took time, one had to be patient. She looked at him, this young man in his swivel chair on the other side of a cluttered desk, and knew that whatever was to be done would not be done by him, or by the cheerful yellow pills like children's sweets.

The daughters came, to inspect and admonish. She said that yes, she had seen the doctor again, and yes, she was feeling rather more . . . herself. She showed them the new sewing-machine with many extra attachments she had not used and when they left she watched them go down the front path to their cars, swinging their bags and shouting at each other, and saw the dog step aside for them, wagging its tail. When they had gone she opened the door and stood there for a few minutes, looking at it, and the dog, five yards away, looked back, not moving.

The next day she took the shopping trolley and set off for the shops. As she opened the front gate she saw the dog come out from the shadow of the fence but she did not turn back. She continued down the street, although she could feel it behind her, keeping its distance. She spoke in a friendly way to a couple of neighbours, did her shopping and returned to the house, and all the while the dog was there, twenty paces off. As she walked to the front door she could hear the click of its claws on the pavement and she had to steel herself so hard not to turn round that when she got inside she was bathed in sweat and shaking all over. When her husband came home that evening he thought her in a funny mood; she asked for a glass of sherry and later suggested they put on a record instead of watching TV – *West Side Story* or another of those shows they went to years ago.

He was surprised at the change in her. She began to go out daily, and although in the evenings she often appeared to be exhausted, as though she had been climbing mountains instead of walking suburban streets, she was curiously calm. Admittedly, she had not appeared agitated before, but her stillness had not been natural; now, he sensed a difference. When the daughters telephoned he reported their mother's condition and listened to their complacent comments; that stuff usually did the trick, they said, all the medics were using it nowadays, they'd always known Mum would be OK soon. But when he put the telephone down and returned to his wife in the sitting room he found himself looking at her uncomfortably. There was an alertness about her that worried him; later, he thought he heard something outside and went to look. He could see nothing at either the front or the back and his wife continued to read a magazine. When he sat down again she looked across at him with a faint smile.

She had started by meeting its eyes, its yellow eyes. And thus she had learned that she could stop it, halt its patient shadowing of her, leave it sitting on the pavement or the garden path. She began to leave the front door ajar, to open the patio window. She could not say what would happen next, knew only that it was inevitable. She no longer sweated or shook; she did not glance behind her when she was outside, and within she hummed to herself as she moved from room to room.

John Case, returning home on an autumn evening, stepped out of the car and saw light streaming through the open front door. He thought he heard his wife speaking to someone in the house. When he came into the kitchen, though, she was alone. He said, 'The front door was open,' and she replied that she must have left it so by mistake. She was busy with a saucepan at the stove and in the corner of the room, her husband saw, was a large dog basket towards which her glance occasionally strayed.

He made no comment. He went back into the hall,

hung up his coat and was startled suddenly by his own face, caught unawares in the mirror by the hatstand and seeming like someone else's – that of a man both older and more burdened than he knew himself to be. He stood staring at it for a few moments and then took a step back towards the kitchen. He could hear the gentle clinking sound of his wife's wooden spoon stirring something in the saucepan and then, he thought, the creak of wickerwork.

He turned sharply and went into the sitting room. He crossed to the window and looked out. He saw the lawn, blackish in the dusk, disappearing into darkness. He switched on the outside lights and flooded it all with an artificial glow – the grass, the little flight of steps up to the patio and the flowerbed at the top of them, from which he had tidied away the spent summer annuals at the weekend. The bare earth was marked all over, he now saw, with what appeared to be animal footprints, and as he stood gazing it seemed to him that he heard the pad of paws on the carpet behind him. He stood for a long while before at last he turned round.

From *Pack of Cards: Stories, 1978–1976*, 2006

✝ As with so many great ghost stories, 'Black Dog' both encourages and evades interpretation. Brenda Case's apparent decision to welcome her black dog, to the point of putting down a basket for it in the kitchen, can be seen as a touching metaphor for how to deal with depression – if that is what the black dog represents. If so, then what is its significance for her husband? And might there be a similar encounter in waiting, somewhere down the line, for those pitilessly positive, no-nonsense daughters?

✝ For all that has been said so far, is there nevertheless something to be said for the rational, common-sense approach to ghostly meetings? 'There are no ghosts', insists editor Ho Chi-Fang in his introduction to a delightful collection of Chinese stories, *Stories About Not Being Afraid of Ghosts*. 'Belief in ghosts is a backward idea, a superstition and a sign of cowardice.' As well he might, given that this collection was published in the People's Republic of China in the years leading up to Chairman Mao's devastating Cultural Revolution. The official line is now that 'the reactionary ruling classes fooled and frightened the people with ghosts and gods so as to strengthen their rule.' Perhaps, but one can't quite avoid the suspicion that Ho Chi-Fang rather enjoys the frisson the evocation of a ghost can create, and that he anticipates his readers relishing that too. In any case, as with 'Black Dog', there's a twist in the tails of these two stories, as related by the Ming Dynasty scholar Lang Ying.

Lang Ying

– Men Take Refuge from Ghosts in a Bath House –

Hunchback Bridge in Hangchow is commonly said to be haunted by evil spirits which molest passers-by. East of the bridge stands a bath house with hot water during the night. One day a man walking alone was caught in the rain. Suddenly he found someone else sharing his umbrella and he suspected this was a ghost. Since they were on the bridge, he pushed the other into the water and took to his heels. Catching sight of a light in the bath house, he went in to escape from the ghost.

Soon a man came in, drenched, who panted, 'A ghost with an umbrella just pushed me into the river so that I was nearly drowned.'

When they talked together, each discovered his mistake.

Another man was out walking one night with no lantern when it was drizzling. Hearing footsteps behind him, he turned and saw a huge head on a body only about two feet tall. He stood still to watch, and the big head stood still too. He walked on, and so did the head. He broke into a run, and the head ran too. In fear and trembling he bolted to the bath house, pushed open the door and dashed in. But before he could close the door the head followed him in, nearly frightening the fellow out of his wits. When he picked up a candle for a better look, it was only a child with a big peck measure on his head to keep off the rain. Because the child was afraid of ghosts too, he had followed closely at his heels. So this man was also mistaken.

Had these four people all gone different ways without clearing the matter up, they would have been convinced that they had seen ghosts. So why should men today think they might see ghosts and be afraid of them?

From *Stories About Not Being Afraid of Ghosts*, 2008,
translated by Yang Hsien-Yi and Gladys Yang

✝ Ghost stories may have plenty to tell us about the experiences of the haunted, but it's rare to find a tale told from the point of view of the ghost itself. If Lang Ying is right, that's hardly surprising; but if ghosts are real, what do they feel? The poet Heine wondered if they might be more afraid of us than we are of them. Ambrose Bierce, the pungent American humourist and creator of *The Devil's Dictionary,* also penned a number of concise, calculatedly shocking 'weird' stories, one of which, 'The Moonlit Road', contains an account apparently dictated through a medium. In that case the element of calculation might be too transparent for some tastes (it is for me); but the story selected here, 'An Occurrence at Owl Creek Bridge', is a very different matter, and this time it's susceptible to more than one interpretation. Bierce's protagonist is a morally ambiguous figure: 'a slave owner and like other slave owners a politician', the author tells us acidly (Bierce was an ardent abolitionist). Yet the sheer animal urgency of his determination to get back to his wife and family, however fantastical, is very compelling. And it leaves a huge question reverberating in our minds: what is it that really happens after Peyton Farquhar's 'awakening' at Owl Creek bridge?

Ambrose Bierce

– An Occurrence at Owl Creek Bridge (1890) –

I

A man stood upon a railroad bridge in northern Alabama, looking down into the swift water twenty feet below. The man's hands were behind his back, the wrists bound with a cord. A rope closely encircled his neck. It was attached to a stout cross-timber above his head and the slack fell to the level of his knees. Some loose boards laid upon the sleepers supporting the metals of the railway supplied a footing for him and his executioners – two private soldiers of the Federal army, directed by a sergeant who in civil life may have been a deputy sheriff. At a short remove upon the same temporary platform was an officer in the uniform of his rank, armed. He was a captain. A sentinel at each end of the bridge stood with his rifle in the position known as 'support', that is to say, vertical in front of the left shoulder, the hammer resting on the forearm thrown straight across the chest – a formal and unnatural position, enforcing an erect carriage of the body. It did not appear to be the duty of these two men to know what was occurring at the center of the bridge; they merely blockaded the two ends of the foot planking that traversed it.

Beyond one of the sentinels nobody was in sight; the railroad ran straight away into a forest for a hundred yards, then, curving, was lost to view. Doubtless there was an outpost farther along. The other bank of the stream was open ground – a gentle acclivity topped with a stockade of vertical tree trunks, loopholed for rifles, with a single embrasure through which protruded the muzzle of a brass cannon commanding the bridge. Midway of the slope between the bridge and fort were the spectators – a single company of infantry in line, at 'parade rest', the butts of the rifles on the ground, the barrels inclining slightly backward against the right shoulder, the hands crossed upon the stock. A lieutenant stood at the right of the line, the point of his sword upon the ground, his left hand resting upon his right. Excepting the group of four at the center of the bridge, not a man moved. The company faced the bridge, staring stonily, motionless. The sentinels, facing the banks of the stream, might have been statues to adorn the bridge. The captain stood with folded arms, silent, observing the work of his subordinates, but making no sign. Death is a dignitary who when he comes announced is to be received with formal manifestations of respect, even by those most familiar with him. In the code of military etiquette silence and fixity are forms of deference.

The man who was engaged in being hanged was apparently about thirty-five years of age. He was a civilian, if one might judge from his habit, which was that of a planter. His features were good – a straight nose, firm mouth, broad forehead, from which his long, dark hair was combed straight back, falling behind his ears to the collar of his well-fitting frock coat. He wore a mustache and pointed beard, but no whiskers; his eyes were large and dark gray, and had a kindly expression which one would hardly have expected in one whose neck was in the hemp. Evidently this was no vulgar assassin. The liberal military code makes provision for hanging many kinds of persons, and gentlemen are not excluded.

The preparations being complete, the two private soldiers stepped aside and each drew away the plank upon which he had been standing. The sergeant turned to the captain, saluted and placed himself immediately behind that officer, who in turn moved apart one pace. These movements left the condemned man and the sergeant standing on the two ends of the same plank, which spanned three of the cross-ties of the bridge. The end upon which the civilian stood almost, but not quite, reached a fourth. This plank had been held in place by the weight of the captain; it was now held by that of the sergeant. At a signal from the former the latter would step aside, the plank would tilt and the condemned man go down between two ties. The arrangement commended itself to his judgment as simple and effective. His face had not been covered nor his eyes bandaged. He looked a moment at his 'unsteadfast footing', then let his gaze wander to the swirling water of the stream racing madly beneath his feet. A piece of dancing driftwood caught his attention and his eyes followed it down the current. How slowly it appeared to move, what a sluggish stream!

He closed his eyes in order to fix his last thoughts upon his wife and children. The water, touched to gold by the early sun, the brooding mists under the banks at some distance down the stream, the fort, the soldiers, the piece of drift – all had distracted him. And now he became conscious of a new disturbance. Striking through the thought of his dear ones was a sound which he could neither ignore nor understand, a sharp, distinct, metallic percussion like the stroke of a blacksmith's hammer upon the anvil; it had the same ringing quality. He wondered what it was, and whether immeasurably distant or nearby – it seemed both. Its recurrence was regular, but as slow as the tolling of a death knell. He awaited each stroke with impatience and – he knew not why – apprehension. The intervals of silence grew progressively longer, the delays became maddening. With their greater infrequency the sounds increased in strength and sharpness. They hurt his ear like the thrust of a knife; he feared he would shriek. What he heard was the ticking of his watch.

He unclosed his eyes and saw again the water below him. 'If I could free my hands,' he thought, 'I might throw off the noose and spring into the stream. By diving I could evade the bullets and, swimming vigorously, reach the bank, take to the woods and get away home. My home, thank God, is as yet outside their lines; my wife and little ones are still beyond the invader's farthest advance.'

As these thoughts, which have here to be set down in words, were flashed into the doomed man's brain rather than evolved from it the captain nodded to the sergeant. The sergeant stepped aside.

II

Peyton Farquhar was a well-to-do planter, of an old and highly respected Alabama family. Being a slave owner and like other slave owners a politician he was naturally an original secessionist and ardently devoted to the Southern cause. Circumstances of an imperious nature, which it is unnecessary to relate here, had prevented him from taking service with the gallant army that had fought the disastrous campaigns ending with the fall of Corinth, and he chafed under the inglorious restraint, longing for the release of his energies, the larger life of the soldier, the opportunity for distinction. That opportunity, he felt, would come, as it comes to all in war time. Meanwhile he did what he could. No service was too humble for him to perform in aid of the South, no adventure too perilous for him to undertake if consistent with the character of a civilian who was at heart a soldier, and who in good faith and without too much qualification assented to at least a part of the frankly villainous dictum that all is fair in love and war.

One evening while Farquhar and his wife were sitting on a rustic bench near the entrance to his grounds, a gray-clad soldier rode up to the gate and asked for a drink of water. Mrs. Farquhar was only too happy to serve him with her own white hands. While she was fetching the water her husband approached the dusty horseman and inquired eagerly for news from the front.

'The Yanks are repairing the railroads,' said the man, 'and are getting ready for another advance. They have reached the Owl Creek bridge, put it in order and built a stockade on the north bank. The commandant has issued an order, which is posted everywhere, declaring that any civilian caught interfering with the railroad, its bridges, tunnels or trains will be summarily hanged. I saw the order.'

'How far is it to the Owl Creek bridge?' Farquhar asked.

'About thirty miles.'

'Is there no force on this side of the creek?'

'Only a picket post half a mile out, on the railroad, and a single sentinel at this end of the bridge.'

'Suppose a man – a civilian and student of hanging – should elude the picket post and perhaps get the better of the sentinel,' said Farquhar, smiling, 'what could he accomplish?'

The soldier reflected. 'I was there a month ago,' he replied. 'I observed that the flood of last winter had lodged a great quantity of driftwood against the wooden pier at this end of the bridge. It is now dry and would burn like tow.'

The lady had now brought the water, which the soldier drank. He thanked her ceremoniously, bowed to her husband and rode away. An hour later, after nightfall, he repassed the plantation, going northward in the direction from which he had come. He was a Federal scout.

III

As Peyton Farquhar fell straight downward through the bridge he lost consciousness and was as one already dead. From this state he was awakened – ages later, it seemed to him – by the pain of a sharp pressure upon his throat, followed by a sense of suffocation. Keen, poignant agonies seemed to shoot from his neck downward through every fiber of his body and limbs. These pains appeared to flash along well-defined lines of ramification and to beat with an inconceivably rapid periodicity. They seemed like streams of pulsating fire heating him to an intolerable temperature. As to his head, he was conscious of nothing but a feeling of fullness – of congestion. These sensations were unaccompanied by thought. The intellectual part of his nature was already effaced; he had power only to feel, and feeling was torment. He was conscious of motion. Encompassed in a luminous cloud, of which he was now merely the fiery heart, without material substance, he swung through unthinkable arcs of oscillation, like a vast pendulum. Then all at once, with terrible suddenness, the light about him shot upward with the noise of a loud splash; a frightful roaring was in his ears, and all was cold and dark. The power of thought was restored; he knew that the rope had broken and he had fallen into the stream. There was no additional strangulation; the noose about his neck was already suffocating him and kept the water from his lungs. To die of hanging at the bottom of a river! – the idea seemed to him ludicrous. He opened his eyes in the darkness and saw above him a gleam of light, but how distant, how inaccessible! He was still sinking, for the light became fainter and fainter until it was a mere glimmer. Then it began to grow and brighten, and he knew that he was rising toward the surface – knew it with reluctance, for he was now very comfortable. 'To be hanged and drowned,' he thought, 'that is not so bad; but I do not wish to be shot. No; I will not be shot; that is not fair.'

He was not conscious of an effort, but a sharp pain in his wrist apprised him that he was trying to free his hands. He gave the struggle his attention, as an idler might observe the feat of a juggler, without interest in the outcome. What splendid effort! – what magnificent, what superhuman strength! Ah, that was a fine endeavor! Bravo! The cord fell away; his arms parted and floated upward, the hands dimly seen on each side in the growing light. He watched them with a new interest as first one and then the other pounced upon the noose at his neck. They tore it away and thrust it fiercely aside, its undulations resembling those of a water snake. 'Put it back, put it back!' He thought he shouted these words to his hands, for the undoing of the noose had been succeeded by the direst pang that he had yet experienced. His neck ached horribly; his brain was on fire; his heart, which had been fluttering faintly, gave a great leap, trying to force itself out at his mouth. His whole body was racked and wrenched with an insupportable anguish! But his disobedient hands gave no heed to the command. They beat the water vigorously with quick, downward strokes, forcing him to the surface. He felt his head emerge; his eyes were blinded by the sunlight; his chest expanded convulsively, and with a supreme and crowning agony his lungs engulfed a great draught of air, which instantly he expelled in a shriek!

He was now in full possession of his physical senses. They were, indeed, preternaturally keen and alert. Something in the awful disturbance of his organic system had so exalted and refined them that they made record of things never before perceived. He felt the ripples upon his face and heard their separate sounds as they struck. He looked at the forest on the bank of the stream, saw the individual trees, the leaves and the veining of each leaf – saw the very insects upon them: the locusts, the brilliant-bodied flies, the grey spiders stretching their webs from twig to twig. He noted the prismatic colors in all the dewdrops upon a million blades of grass. The humming of the gnats that danced above the eddies of the stream, the beating of the dragon flies' wings, the strokes of the water-spiders' legs, like oars which had lifted their boat – all these made audible music. A fish slid along beneath his eyes and he heard the rush of its body parting the water.

He had come to the surface facing down the stream; in a moment the visible world seemed to wheel slowly round, himself the pivotal point, and he saw the bridge, the fort, the soldiers upon the bridge, the captain, the sergeant, the two privates, his executioners. They were in silhouette against the blue sky. They shouted and gesticulated, pointing at him. The captain had drawn his pistol, but did not fire; the others were unarmed. Their movements were grotesque and horrible, their forms gigantic.

Suddenly he heard a sharp report and something struck the water smartly within a few inches of his head, spattering his face with spray. He heard a second report, and saw one of the sentinels with his rifle at his shoulder, a light cloud of blue smoke rising from the muzzle. The man in the water saw the eye of the man on the bridge gazing into his own through the sights of the rifle. He observed that it was a gray eye and remembered having read that gray eyes were keenest, and that all famous marksmen had them. Nevertheless, this one had missed. A counter-swirl had caught Farquhar and turned him half round; he was again looking into the forest on the bank opposite the fort. The sound of a clear, high voice in a monotonous singsong now rang out behind him and came across the water with a distinctness that pierced and subdued all other sounds, even the beating of the ripples in his ears. Although no soldier, he had frequented camps enough to know the dread significance of that deliberate, drawling, aspirated chant; the lieutenant on shore was taking a part in the morning's work. How coldly and pitilessly – with what an even, calm intonation, presaging, and enforcing tranquillity in the men – with what accurately measured intervals fell those cruel words:

'Attention, company! . . . Shoulder arms! . . . Ready! . . . Aim! . . . Fire!'

Farquhar dived – dived as deeply as he could. The water roared in his ears like the voice of Niagara, yet he heard the dulled thunder of the volley and, rising again toward the surface, met shining bits of metal, singularly flattened, oscillating slowly downward. Some of them touched him on the face and hands, then fell away, continuing their descent. One lodged between his collar and neck; it was uncomfortably warm and he snatched it out.

As he rose to the surface, gasping for breath, he saw that he had been a long time under water; he was perceptibly farther downstream nearer to safety.

The soldiers had almost finished reloading; the metal ramrods flashed all at once in the sunshine as they were drawn from the barrels, turned in the air, and thrust into their sockets. The two sentinels fired again, independently and ineffectually.

The hunted man saw all this over his shoulder; he was now swimming vigorously with the current. His brain was as energetic as his arms and legs; he thought with the rapidity of lightning.

'The officer,' he reasoned, 'will not make that martinet's error a second time. It is as easy to dodge a volley as a single shot. He has probably already given the command to fire at will. God help me, I cannot dodge them all!'

An appalling splash within two yards of him was followed by a loud, rushing sound, diminuendo, which seemed to travel back through the air to the fort and died in an explosion which stirred the very river to its deeps!

A rising sheet of water curved over him, fell down upon him, blinded him, strangled him! The cannon had taken a hand in the game. As he shook his head free from the commotion of the smitten water he heard the deflected shot humming through the air ahead, and in an instant it was cracking and smashing the branches in the forest beyond.

'They will not do that again,' he thought; 'the next time they will use a charge of grape. I must keep my eye upon the gun; the smoke will apprise me – the report arrives too late; it lags behind the missile. That is a good gun.'

Suddenly he felt himself whirled round and round – spinning like a top. The water, the banks, the forests, the now distant bridge, fort and men – all were commingled and blurred. Objects were represented by their colors only; circular horizontal streaks of color – that was all he saw. He had been caught in a vortex and was being whirled on with a velocity of advance and gyration that made him giddy and sick. In a few moments he was flung upon the gravel at the foot of the left bank of the stream – the southern bank – and behind a projecting point which concealed him from his enemies. The sudden arrest of his motion, the abrasion of one of his hands on the gravel, restored him, and he wept with delight. He dug his fingers into the sand, threw it over himself in handfuls and audibly blessed it. It looked like diamonds, rubies, emeralds; he could think of nothing beautiful which it did not resemble. The trees upon the bank were giant garden plants; he noted a definite order in their arrangement, inhaled the fragrance of their blooms. A strange, roseate light shone through the spaces among their trunks and the wind made in their branches the music of Aeolian harps. He had no wish to perfect his escape – was content to remain in that enchanting spot until retaken.

A whiz and rattle of grapeshot among the branches high above his head roused him from his dream. The baffled cannoneer had fired him a random farewell. He sprang to his feet, rushed up the sloping bank, and plunged into the forest.

All that day he traveled, laying his course by the rounding sun. The forest seemed interminable; nowhere did he discover a break in it, not even a woodman's road. He had not known that he lived in so wild a region. There was something uncanny in the revelation.

By nightfall he was fatigued, footsore, famishing. The thought of his wife and children urged him on. At last he found a road which led him in what he knew to be the right direction. It was as wide and straight as a city street, yet it seemed untraveled. No fields bordered it, no dwelling anywhere. Not so much as the barking of a dog suggested human habitation. The black bodies of the trees formed a straight wall on both sides, terminating on the horizon in a point, like a diagram in a lesson in perspective. Overhead, as he looked up through this rift in the wood, shone great garden stars looking unfamiliar and grouped in strange constellations. He was sure they were arranged in some order which had a secret and malign significance. The wood on either side was full of singular noises, among which – once, twice, and again – he distinctly heard whispers in an unknown tongue.

His neck was in pain and lifting his hand to it found it horribly swollen. He knew that it had a circle of black where the rope had bruised it. His eyes felt congested;

he could no longer close them. His tongue was swollen with thirst; he relieved its fever by thrusting it forward from between his teeth into the cold air. How softly the turf had carpeted the untraveled avenue – he could no longer feel the roadway beneath his feet!

Doubtless, despite his suffering, he had fallen asleep while walking, for now he sees another scene – perhaps he has merely recovered from a delirium. He stands at the gate of his own home. All is as he left it, and all bright and beautiful in the morning sunshine. He must have traveled the entire night. As he pushes open the gate and passes up the wide white walk, he sees a flutter of female garments; his wife, looking fresh and cool and sweet, steps down from the veranda to meet him. At the bottom of the steps she stands waiting, with a smile of ineffable joy, an attitude of matchless grace and dignity. Ah, how beautiful she is! He springs forward with extended arms. As he is about to clasp her he feels a stunning blow upon the back of the neck; a blinding white light blazes all about him with a sound like the shock of a cannon – then all is darkness and silence!

Peyton Farquhar was dead; his body, with a broken neck, swung gently from side to side beneath the timbers of the Owl Creek bridge.

From *Tales of Soldiers and Civilians*, 1891

✝ So, is it all a dream, unfolding in the haunted chambers of Peyton Farquhar's brain in the split seconds before the hangman's rope does its grisly job? Or does he actually achieve the impossible and somehow raise that 'smile of ineffable joy' on his already bereaved wife's face? That was the inference drawn by the composer Thea Musgrave in her chamber opera *An Occurrence at Owl Creek Bridge* (1981) based on Bierce's story, and very moving it is too. Bierce, however, prefers to leave us in doubt.

✝ The 'anonymous' motto that heads W. W. Jacobs' 'The Monkey's Paw' says just about all that needs to be said about the moral of this concise and devastating tale – for the moment at least. It has been much anthologised, and adapted many times into different media, but it loses none of its power on repetition. In fact for modern readers, coming to terms with the radical shifts in perspective brought about by post-colonial criticism, there may be still more uncomfortable resonances.

W. W. Jacobs

– The Monkey's Paw (1902) –

'Be careful what you wish for, you may receive it.'
– Anonymous

PART ONE

Outside, the night was cold and wet, but in the small living room the curtains were closed and the fire burned brightly. Father and son were playing chess; the father, whose ideas about the game involved some very unusual moves, putting his king into such sharp and unnecessary danger that it even brought comment from the white-haired old lady knitting quietly by the fire.

'Listen to the wind,' said Mr. White who, having seen a mistake that could cost him the game after it was too late, was trying to stop his son from seeing it.

'I'm listening,' said the son, seriously studying the board as he stretched out his hand. 'Check.'

'I should hardly think that he'll come tonight,' said his father, with his hand held in the air over the board.

'Mate,' replied the son.

'That's the worst of living so far out,' cried Mr. White with sudden and unexpected violence; 'Of all the awful out of the way places to live in, this is the worst. Can't walk on the footpath without getting stuck in the mud, and the road's a river. I don't know what the people are thinking about. I suppose they think it doesn't matter because only two houses in the road have people in them.'

'Never mind, dear,' said his wife calmly; 'perhaps you'll win the next one.'

Mr. White looked up sharply, just in time to see a knowing look between mother and son. The words died away on his lips, and he hid a guilty smile in his thin grey beard.

'There he is,' said Herbert White as the gate banged shut loudly and heavy footsteps came toward the door.

The old man rose quickly and opening the door, was heard telling the new arrival how sorry he was for his recent loss. The new arrival talked about his sadness, so that Mrs. White said, 'Tut, tut!' and coughed gently as her husband entered the room followed by a tall, heavy built, strong-looking man, whose skin had the healthy reddish colour associated with outdoor life and whose eyes showed that he could be a dangerous enemy.

'Sergeant-Major Morris,' he said, introducing him to his wife and his son, Herbert.

The Sergeant-Major shook hands and, taking the offered seat by the fire, watched with satisfaction as Mr. White got out whiskey and glasses.

After the third glass his eyes got brighter and he began to talk. The little family circle listened with growing interest to this visitor from distant parts, as he squared his broad shoulders in the chair and spoke of wild scenes and brave acts; of wars and strange peoples.

'Twenty-one years of it,' said Mr. White, looking at his wife and son. 'When he went away he was a thin young man. Now look at him.'

'He doesn't look to have taken much harm,' said Mrs. White politely.

'I'd like to go to India myself,' said the old man, just to look around a bit, you know.'

'Better where you are,' said the Sergeant-Major, shaking his head. He put down the empty glass and sighing softly, shook it again.

'I should like to see those old temples and fakirs and the street entertainers,' said the old man. 'What was that that you started telling me the other day about a monkey's paw or something, Morris?'

'Nothing,' said the soldier quickly. 'At least, nothing worth hearing.'

'Monkey's paw?' said Mrs. White curiously.

'Well, it's just a bit of what you might call magic, perhaps,' said the Sergeant-Major, without first stopping to think.

His three listeners leaned forward excitedly. Deep in thought, the visitor put his empty glass to his lips and then set it down again. Mr. White filled it for him again.

'To look at it,' said the Sergeant-Major, feeling

about in his pocket, 'it's just an ordinary little paw, dried to a mummy.'

He took something out of his pocket and held it out for them. Mrs. White drew back with a look of disgust, but her son, taking it, examined it curiously.

'And what is there special about it?' asked Mr. White as he took it from his son, and having examined it, placed it upon the table.

'It had a spell put on it by an old fakir,' said the Sergeant-Major, 'a very holy man. He wanted to show that fate ruled people's lives, and that those who tried to change it would be sorry. He put a spell on it so that three different men could each have three wishes from it.'

The way he told the story showed that he truly believed it and his listeners became aware that their light laughter was out of place and had hurt him a little.

'Well, why don't you have three, sir?' said Herbert, cleverly.

The soldier looked at him the way that the middle aged usually look at disrespectful youth. 'I have,' he said quietly, and his face whitened.

'And did you really have the three wishes granted?' asked Mrs. White.

'I did,' said the Sergeant-Major, and his glass tapped against his strong teeth.

'And has anybody else wished?' continued the old lady.

'The first man had his three wishes. Yes,' was the

reply. 'I don't know what the first two were, but the third was for death. That's how I got the paw.'

His voice was so serious that the group fell quiet.

'If you've had your three wishes it's no good to you now then Morris,' said the old man at last. 'What do you keep it for?'

The soldier shook his head. 'Fancy I suppose,' he said slowly. 'I did have some idea of selling it, but I don't think I will. It has caused me enough trouble already. Besides, people won't buy. They think it's just a story, some of them; and those who do think anything of it want to try it first and pay me afterward.'

'If you could have another three wishes,' said the old man, watching him carefully, 'would you have them?'

'I don't know,' said the other. 'I don't know.'

He took the paw, and holding it between his front finger and thumb, suddenly threw it upon the fire. Mr. White, with a slight cry, quickly bent down and took it off.

'Better let it burn,' said the soldier sadly, but in a way that let them know he believed it to be true.

'If you don't want it Morris,' said the other, 'give it to me.'

'I won't,' said his friend with stubborn determination. 'I threw it on the fire. If you keep it, don't hold me responsible for what happens. Throw it on the fire like a sensible man.'

The other shook his head and examined his possession closely. 'How do you do it?' he asked.

'Hold it up in your right hand, and state your wish out loud so that you can be heard,' said the Sergeant-Major. 'But I warn you of what might happen.'

'Sounds like the *Arabian Nights*,' said Mrs. White, as she rose and began to set the dinner. 'Don't you think you might wish for four pairs of hands for me.'

Her husband drew the talisman from his pocket, and all three laughed loudly as the Sergeant-Major, with a look of alarm on his face, caught him by the arm.

'If you must wish,' he demanded, 'wish for something sensible.'

Mr. White dropped it back in his pocket, and placing chairs, motioned his friend to the table. In the business of dinner the talisman was partly forgotten, and afterward the three sat fascinated as they listened to more of the soldier's adventures in India.

'If the tale about the monkey's paw is not more truthful than those he has been telling us,' said Herbert, as the door closed behind their guest, just in time to catch the last train, 'we shan't make much out of it.'

'Did you give anything for it, father?' asked Mrs. White, watching her husband closely.

'A little,' said he, colouring slightly. 'He didn't want it, but I made him take it. And he pressed me again to throw it away.'

'Not likely!' said Herbert, with pretended horror. 'Why, we're going to be rich, and famous, and happy.'

Smiling, he said, 'Wish to be a king, father, to begin with; then mother can't complain all the time.'

He ran quickly around the table, chased by the laughing Mrs. White armed with a piece of cloth.

Mr. White took the paw from his pocket and eyed it doubtfully. 'I don't know what to wish for, and that's a fact,' he said slowly. 'It seems to me I've got all I want.'

'If you only paid off the house, you'd be quite happy, wouldn't you!' said Herbert, with his hand on his shoulder. 'Well, wish for two hundred pounds, then; that'll just do it.'

His father, smiling and with an embarrassed look for his foolishness in believing the soldier's story, held up the talisman. Herbert, with a serious face, spoiled only by a quick smile to his mother, sat down at the piano and struck a few grand chords.

'I wish for two hundred pounds,' said the old man clearly.

A fine crash from the piano greeted his words, broken by a frightened cry from the old man. His wife and son ran toward him.

'It moved,' he cried, with a look of horror at the object as it lay on the floor. 'As I wished, it twisted in my hand like a snake.'

'Well, I don't see the money,' said his son, as he picked it up and placed it on the table, 'and I bet I never shall.'

'It must have been your imagination, father,' said his wife, regarding him worriedly.

He shook his head. 'Never mind, though; there's no harm done, but it gave me a shock all the same.'

They sat down by the fire again while the two men finished their pipes. Outside, the wind was higher than ever, and the old man jumped nervously at the sound of a door banging upstairs. An unusual and depressing silence settled on all three, which lasted until the old couple got up to go to bed.

'I expect you'll find the cash tied up in a big bag in the middle of your bed,' said Herbert, as he wished them goodnight, 'and something horrible sitting on top of your wardrobe watching you as you pocket your ill-gotten money.'

Herbert, who normally had a playful nature and didn't like to take things too seriously, sat alone in the darkness looking into the dying fire. He saw faces in it; the last so horrible and so monkey-like that he stared at it in amazement. It became so clear that, with a nervous laugh, he felt on the table for a glass containing some water to throw over it. His hand found the monkey's paw, and with a little shake of his body he wiped his hand on his coat and went up to bed.

PART TWO

In the brightness of the wintry sun the next morning as it streamed over the breakfast table he laughed at his fears. The room felt as it always had and there was an air of health and happiness which was not there the previous night. The dirty, dried-up little paw was thrown on the cabinet with a carelessness which indicated no great belief in what good it could do.

'I suppose all old soldiers are the same,' said Mrs. White. 'The idea of our listening to such nonsense! How could wishes be granted in these days? And if they could, how could two hundred pounds hurt you, father?'

'Might drop on his head from the sky,' said Herbert.

'Morris said the things happened so naturally,' said his father, 'that you might if you so wished not see the relationship.'

'Well don't break into the money before I come back,' said Herbert as he rose from the table to go to work. 'I'm afraid it'll turn you into a mean, greedy old man, and we shall have to tell everyone that we don't know you.'

His mother laughed, and following him to the door, watched him go down the road, and returning to the breakfast table, she felt very happy at the expense of her husband's readiness to believe such stories. All of which did not prevent her from hurrying to the door at the postman's knock nor, when she found that the post brought only a bill, talking about how Sergeant-Majors can develop bad drinking habits after they leave the army.

'Herbert will have some more of his funny remarks, I expect, when he comes home,' she said as they sat at dinner.

'I know,' said Mr. White, pouring himself out some beer; 'but for all that, the thing moved in my hand; that I'll swear to.'

'You thought it did,' said the old lady, trying to calm him.

'I say it did,' replied the other. 'There was no thought about it; I had just – What's the matter?'

His wife made no reply. She was watching the mysterious movements of a man outside, who, looking in an undecided fashion at the house, appeared to be trying to make up his mind to enter. In mental connection with the two hundred pounds, she noticed that the stranger was well dressed, and wore a silk hat of shiny newness. Three times he stopped briefly at the gate, and then walked on again. The fourth time he stood with his hand upon it, and then with sudden firmness of mind pushed it open and walked up the path. Mrs. White at the same moment placed her hands behind her, hurriedly untied the strings of her apron, and put it under the cushion of her chair.

She brought the stranger, who seemed a little uncomfortable, into the room. He looked at her in a way that said there was something about his purpose that he wanted to keep secret, and seemed to be thinking of something else as the old lady said she was sorry for the appearance of the room and her husband's coat, which he usually wore in the garden. She then waited as patiently as her sex would permit for him to state his business, but he was at first strangely silent.

'I – was asked to call,' he said at last, and bent down and picked a piece of cotton from his trousers. 'I come from Maw and Meggins.'

The old lady jumped suddenly, as in alarm. 'Is anything the matter?' she asked breathlessly. 'Has anything happened to Herbert? What is it? What is it?'

Her husband spoke before he could answer. 'There there mother,' he said hurriedly. 'Sit down, and don't jump to a conclusion. You've not brought bad news, I'm sure sir,' and eyed the other, expecting that it was bad news but hoping he was wrong.

'I'm sorry – ' began the visitor.

'Is he hurt?' demanded the mother wildly.

The visitor lowered and raised his head once in agreement. 'Badly hurt,' he said quietly, 'but he is not in any pain.'

'Oh thank God!' said the old woman, pressing her hands together tightly. 'Thank God for that! Thank – '

She broke off as the tragic meaning of the part about him not being in pain came to her. The man had turned his head slightly so as not to look directly at her, but she saw the awful truth in his face. She caught her breath, and turning to her husband, who did not yet understand the man's meaning, laid her shaking hand on his. There was a long silence.

'He was caught in the machinery,' said the visitor at length in a low voice.

'Caught in the machinery,' repeated Mr. White, too shocked to think clearly, 'yes.'

He sat staring out the window, and taking his wife's hand between his own, pressed it as he used to do when he was trying to win her love in the time before they were married, nearly forty years before.

'He was the only one left to us,' he said, turning gently to the visitor. 'It is hard.'

The other coughed, and rising, walked slowly to the window. 'The firm wishes me to pass on their great sadness about your loss,' he said, without looking round. 'I ask that you please understand that I am only their servant and simply doing what they told me to do.'

There was no reply; the old woman's face was white, her eyes staring, and her breath unheard; on the husband's face was a look such as his friend the Sergeant-Major might have carried into his first battle.

'I was to say that Maw and Meggins accept no responsibility,' continued the other. 'But, although they don't believe that they have a legal requirement to make a payment to you for your loss, in view of your son's services they wish to present you with a certain sum.'

Mr. White dropped his wife's hand, and rising to his feet, stared with a look of horror at his visitor. His dry lips shaped the words, 'How much?'

'Two hundred pounds,' was the answer.

Without hearing his wife's scream, the old man smiled weakly, put out his hands like a blind man, and fell, a senseless mass, to the floor.

PART THREE

In the huge new cemetery, some two miles away, the old people buried their dead, and came back to the house which was now full of shadows and silence. It was all over so quickly that at first they could hardly realize it, and remained in a state of waiting for something else to happen – something else which was to lighten this load, too heavy for old hearts to bear.

But the days passed, and they realized that they had to accept the situation – the hopeless acceptance of the old. Sometimes they hardly said a word to each other, for now they had nothing to talk about, and their days were long to tiredness.

It was about a week after that the old man, waking suddenly in the night, stretched out his hand and found himself alone. The room was in darkness, and he could hear the sound of his wife crying quietly at the window. He raised himself in bed and listened.

'Come back,' he said tenderly. 'You will be cold.'

'It is colder for my son,' said the old woman, who began crying again.

The sounds of crying died away on his ears. The bed was warm, and his eyes heavy with sleep. He slept lightly at first, and then was fully asleep until a sudden wild cry from his wife woke him with a start.

'THE PAW!' she cried wildly. 'THE MONKEY'S PAW!'

He started up in alarm. 'Where? Where is it?

What's the matter?'

She almost fell as she came hurried across the room toward him. 'I want it,' she said quietly. 'You've not destroyed it?'

'It's in the living room, on the shelf above the fire-place,' he replied. 'Why?'

She cried and laughed together, and bending over, kissed his cheek.

'I only just thought of it,' she said. 'Why didn't I think of it before? Why didn't you think of it?'

'Think of what?' he questioned.

'The other two wishes,' she replied quickly. 'We've only had one.'

'Was not that enough?' he demanded angrily.

'No,' she cried excitedly; 'We'll have one more. Go down and get it quickly, and wish our boy alive again.'

The man sat up in bed and threw the blankets from his shaking legs. 'Good God, you are mad!' he cried, struck with horror.

'Get it,' she said, breathing quickly; 'get it quickly, and wish – Oh my boy, my boy!'

Her husband struck a match and lit the candle. 'Get back to bed he said,' his voice shaking. 'You don't know what you are saying.'

'We had the first wish granted,' said the old wom-an, desperately; 'why not the second?'

'A c-c-coincidence,' said the old man.

'Go get it and wish,' cried his wife, shaking with excitement.

The old man turned and looked at her, and his voice shook. 'He has been dead ten days, and besides he – I would not tell you before, but – I could only recognize him by his clothing. If he was too terrible for you to see then, how now?'

'Bring him back,' cried the old woman, and pulled him towards the door. 'Do you think I fear the child I have nursed?'

He went down in the darkness, and felt his way to the living room, and then to the fireplace. The talisman was in its place on the shelf, and then a horrible fear came over him that the unspoken wish might bring the broken body of his son before him before he could escape from the room. He caught his breath as he found that he had lost the direction of the door. His forehead cold with sweat, he felt his way round the table and along the walls until he found himself at the bottom of the stairs with the evil thing in his hand.

Even his wife's face seemed changed as he entered the room. It was white and expectant, and to his fears seemed to have an unnatural look upon it. He was afraid of her.

'WISH!' she cried in a strong voice.

'It is foolish and wicked,' he said weakly.

'WISH!' repeated his wife.

He raised his hand. 'I wish my son alive again.'

The talisman fell to the floor, and he looked at it fearfully. Then he sank into a chair and the old woman, with burning eyes, walked to the window and opened the curtains.

He sat until he could no longer bear the cold, looking up from time to time at the figure of his wife staring through the window. The candle, which had almost burned to the bottom, was throwing moving shadows around the room. When the candle finally went out, the old man, with an unspeakable sense of relief at the failure of the talisman, went slowly back to his bed, and a minute afterward the old woman came silently and lay without movement beside him.

Neither spoke, but lay silently listening to the ticking of the clock. They heard nothing else other than the normal night sounds. The darkness was depressing, and after lying for some time building up his courage, the husband took the box of matches, and lighting one, went downstairs for another candle.

At the foot of the stairs the match went out, and he stopped to light another; and at the same moment a knock sounded on the front door. It was so quiet that it could only be heard downstairs, as if the one knocking wanted to keep their coming a secret.

The matches fell from his hand. He stood motionless, not even breathing, until the knock was repeated. Then he turned and ran quickly back to his room, and closed the door behind him. A third knock sounded through the house.

'WHAT'S THAT?' cried the old woman, sitting up quickly.

'A rat,' said the old man shakily, 'a rat. It passed me on the stairs.'

His wife sat up in bed listening. A loud knock echoed through the house. 'It's Herbert!' she screamed. 'It's Herbert!'

She ran to the door, but her husband was there before her, and catching her by the arm, held her tightly. 'What are you going to do?' he asked in a low, scared voice.

'It's my boy; it's Herbert!' she cried, struggling automatically. 'I forgot it was two miles away. What are you holding me for? Let go. I must open the door.'

'For God's sake don't let it in,' cried the old man, shaking with fear.

'You're afraid of your own son,' she cried struggling. 'Let me go. I'm coming, Herbert; I'm coming.'

There was another knock, and another. The old woman with a sudden pull broke free and ran from the room. Her husband followed to the top of the stairs, and called after her as she hurried down. He heard the chain pulled back and the bottom lock open. Then the old woman's voice, desperate and breathing heavily.

'The top lock,' she cried loudly. 'Come down. I can't reach it.'

✝ Western materialism and acquisitiveness, the greed that leads to empire-building, come up against ancient wisdom, and are finally destroyed by it – that's one possible way of reading the message of 'The Monkey's Paw'. Even so, it's hard not to be stirred to compassion for Mr. and Mrs. White. Did Nemesis have to be quite so cruel? We seem to have strayed beyond Tove Jansson's notion of 'menacing enchantment' into somewhere far more terrible. But Jansson herself provides a wonderful example of how the themes of desolation and compassion can ultimately yield a more hopeful message, and we find it in an unlikely source. There is a ghost in Tove Jansson's glorious Moomin stories, but he's a harmless, gentle creature, not at all frightening, and no stranger than any of the other fabulous creatures in Jansson's classic children's tales. But there is also the truly spectral Groke, subject of many an infant nightmare: menacing, nocturnal, always leaving behind her a trail of ice. In the penultimate Moomin book, *Moominpappa at Sea*, she follows the Moomin family as they set off for their summer holiday on a small island in the Baltic Sea. Young Moomintroll realises she is there, floating on a tiny ice island in the darkness, as he makes his nightly trip to hang out the hurricane lamp. At first he's paralysed: 'He wanted to go away from the coldness and motionlessness of her, far away from the terrifying loneliness of her. But he couldn't move.' On later visits, she draws nearer, entranced by the lamp: entranced to the point where – can it be that she's actually dancing? Then comes the moment when she takes her eyes off the lamp for the first time and stares at Moomintroll: 'She had such cold eyes, and they looked so anxious.'

Perhaps Heine was right after all. Before long, something similar begins to dawn on Moomintroll.

Tove Jansson

– *from* Moominpappa at Sea (1986) –

'Moomintroll and the Groke'

After he had taken Moominmamma home, Moomintroll put out the hurricane lamp. He wanted to be alone. The wind was getting up. The darkness, the thundering of the sea, and something that Moominmamma had said, made him feel safe.

He came to the place where the rock fell away towards the black pool. He could hear the sound of the water splashing at the bottom of the cliff, but he didn't stop. He strolled on, feeling as light as a balloon and not the least bit sleepy.

And then he saw her. The Groke had come right up on to the island and she was nosing around below the lighthouse-rock. There she was, shuffling up and down, sniffing in the heather, and staring short-sightedly all round her. Then she wandered off towards the swamp.

'She's looking for me,' thought Moomintroll. 'But she might as well take it easy. I'm not going to light the lamp, it takes too much paraffin.'

He stood still for a moment, watching her wander forlornly over the island.

'She can dance tomorrow night,' he said to himself

with a feeling of kindly indulgence. 'But not just now. I feel like staying at home tonight.'

So he turned his back on the Groke and took a roundabout route back to his glade.

Moomintroll woke at dawn with a feeling of panic. He was shut in. He was suffocating inside his sleeping bag. Something was holding him down and he couldn't get his paws out. Everything felt upside down and he was surrounded by a curious brown light and a strange smell, as though he was deep down in the earth.

At last he managed to loosen the zip of his sleeping bag. A cloud of soil and pine needles was whirling round him, the whole world seemed changed, and he felt utterly lost. Everywhere, brown roots were creeping along the ground and right over his sleeping bag. The trees weren't actually moving now, but in the darkness they had moved away from above his head. The whole forest had pulled up its root and stepped over him just as though he was a stone. There was the matchbox just where it always was and next to it the bottle of blackcurrant juice. But the glade had gone – it just wasn't there any more. The tunnels he had made had all grown over again. He seemed to be in a primeval forest, fleeing with the trees, creeping along the ground, dragging his sleeping bag. He had to hold on to it because it was a very fine sleeping bag, and, besides, it had been given to him as a present.

He caught sight of the hurricane lamp. It was

hanging in the tree where he had put it, but the tree had moved.

Moomintroll sat down and screamed for Little My at the top of his voice. She answered immediately. She gave a long series of signals in a voice that sounded like the clarion calls of a very small trumpet, or a buoy far out at sea. Moomintroll started to crawl in the direction of the sound.

He came out into the daylight and the wind blew right in his face. He got up, his legs shaking, and looked at Little My with a feeling of intense relief. He thought that for once she was almost pretty.

A few of the smaller bushes which had pulled their roots out of the ground without any difficulty were already lying tangled and confused in the heather some way off. The swampy patch had sunk right into the ground and looked like a deep green ravine.

'What's happening?' Moomintroll cried. 'Why are they pulling up their roots like that? I don't understand it.'

'They're scared stiff,' said Little My, looking at him right between the eyes. 'They're so scared that every little pine-needle is standing on end. They're even more scared than you are! If I didn't know that in fact it's the other way round, I should think that the Groke had been here. Eh?'

Moomintroll felt a sinking feeling in his tummy and sat down in the heather. The heather was just the same as ever, thank goodness! It was flowering just as usual, and had decided to stay just where it was.

'The Groke,' continued Little My thoughtfully. 'Big, and cold, and wandering around, sitting down all over the place. And do you know what happens when she sits down?' Of course he knew. Nothing would grow. Nothing would ever grow where she had sat.

'Why are you staring at me like that?' Moomintroll exclaimed.

'Was I staring at you?' asked Little My innocently. 'Why should I? Perhaps I was staring at something behind you . . .'

Moomintroll jumped up and looked around, terrified.

'Ha, ha! I was only pulling your leg!' cried Little My, delighted. 'Isn't it funny how a whole island can go off its rocker and start moving? I think it's jolly interesting.'

But Moomintroll didn't think it was funny. The thicket was moving towards the lighthouse, right across the island towards the lighthouse steps. It would get a little nearer every night until the first low-lying branch was pushing against the door and trying to get in.

'We won't open the door!' he said. Suddenly he looked at Little My right between the eyes. They were jolly eyes and they seemed to be laughing at him, as if to say: 'I know all your secrets.'

Somehow, this made him feel a lot better.

[. . .] At dusk Moomintroll went to fill the hurricane lamp.

The can of paraffin was underneath the stairs with a pile of torn nets. He put a tin under the hole in the top and took out the stopper. When he lifted the can it rattled, making a strange echoing sound. He held it over the tin and waited. He shook the can.

Then he put it down and stood staring at the floor for a moment. There was no more paraffin. It was finished. The lamp had been burning every night in the room upstairs and every night he had shone it for the Groke. Apart from that Little My had poured several pints over the ants. What was he to do? What would the Groke say? He daren't think how disappointed she would be. He sat down on the stairs with his nose in his paws.

He felt as though he had let her down.

'Are you absolutely certain the whole can's empty?' Moominmamma asked, giving the lamp a good shake.

They had finished their tea, and the windows were getting dark.

'Quite empty,' said Moomintroll wretchedly.

'It must be leaking,' said Moominpappa. 'Perhaps it's getting rusty. It's impossible that we've used all that paraffin.'

Moominmamma sighed. 'Now we shall have to manage with the light of the fire in the stove,' she said. 'There are only three candles left and I must put them on the fisherman's birthday cake.' She put some more wood on the fire and left the door of the stove open.

The fire crackled cheerfully, and the family pulled the boxes in a small semi-circle round it. From time to time the storm whistled in the chimney. It was a lonely, melancholy sound.

'I wonder what's happening outside?' said Moominmamma.

'I can tell you,' Moominpappa answered. 'The island is going to bed. I can assure you that it's going to bed and will go to sleep at about the same time as we do.'

Moominmamma laughed a little. Then she said thoughtfully: 'Do you know, all the time we've been living here like this, I've had the feeling that we're on an expedition somewhere. Everything is so different all the time, as if it was Sunday every day. I'm beginning to wonder whether it's a good feeling after all.'

The others waited for her to go on.

'Of course we can't always be on an expedition. It has to come to an end sometime. I'm terribly afraid that it will suddenly feel like Monday again and then I shan't be able to feel that any of this has been real . . .' She was silent and looked at Moominpappa a little hesitatingly.

'But of course it's real,' said Moominpappa, amazed. 'And it's fine to feel that it's always Sunday. It's just that feeling that we had lost.'

'What *are* you talking about?' asked Little My.

Moomintroll stretched his legs. He had a feeling too, all over. He could only think of the Groke. 'I think I'll go outside for a little while,' he said.

The others looked at him.

'I want a breath of fresh air,' he said impatiently. 'I can't sit here stewing any longer. I need some exercise.'

'Now, listen,' Moominpappa began, but Moominmamma said, 'All right, go outside if you feel like it.'

'What's come over him?' asked Moominpappa when Moomintroll had gone.

'It's growing pains,' said Moominmamma. 'He doesn't understand what's wrong with him either. You never seem to realise that he's growing up. You seem to think he's still a little child.'

'Of course he's still quite small,' said Moominpappa, somewhat surprised.

Moominmamma laughed and poked the fire. It was really much nicer than candlelight.

The Groke sat waiting on the beach. Moomintroll came towards her without the hurricane lamp. He stopped by the boat and looked at her. There was nothing he could do for her.

He could hear the beating of the island's heart, and the sound of the stones and the trees moving slowly away from the sea. There was nothing he could do to stop it.

Suddenly the Groke started to sing. Her skirts fluttered as she swayed to and fro, stamping on the sand and doing her best to show him that she was pleased to see him.

Moomintroll moved forwards in amazement. There was no doubt about it, the Groke was pleased to see him. She didn't mind about the hurricane lamp. She was delighted that he had come to meet her.

He stood quite still until she had finished her dance. Then he watched her shuffle off down the beach and disappear. He went and felt the sand where she had stood. It wasn't frozen hard at all, but felt the same as it always did. He listened carefully, but all he could hear was the breakers. It was as if the island had suddenly fallen asleep.

He went back home. The others were already in bed, and there were only a few glowing embers in the stove. He crept into bed and curled up.

'What did she say?' asked Little My.

'She was pleased,' Moomintroll whispered back. 'She didn't notice any difference.'

From *Moominpappa at Sea*, 1965, translated by Kingsley Hart, 1950

✝ It is compassion, then, which helps Moomintroll put his ghost to rest in *Moominpappa at Sea* – Jansson's stories are full of such moments of tender wisdom, learned, one suspects, from hard personal experience. We may also remember how compassion briefly overcame alarm for Lockwood in *Wuthering Heights* when he saws Heathcliff's agonised grief. As he listens to the tale of the tragic lovers, related by the housekeeper Nelly Dean, there are moments when one senses that compassion flickering again. At the end, when the story is told – and how often in these tales the act of storytelling is integral to the plot, and unquestionably to its cathartic effect – we sense a powerful contrast. For the locals, it would seem a simple, literal truth that 'the evil that men do lives after them'; but for Lockwood, brought by Nelly's narration far closer to the heart of the matter, the outcome is rather different. First she rounds off her story with the recent shocking news of Heathcliff's death.

Emily Brontë

– *from* Wuthering Heights (1847) –

T he following evening was very wet: indeed, it poured down till day-dawn; and, as I took my morning walk round the house, I observed the master's window swinging open, and the rain driving straight in.

'He cannot be in bed', I thought, 'those showers would drench him through. He must either be up or out. But I'll make no more ado, I'll go boldly and look!'

Having succeeded in obtaining entrance with another key, I ran to unclose the panels, for the chamber was vacant; quickly pushing them aside, I peeped in. Mr. Heathcliff was there – laid on his back. His eyes met mine so keen and fierce, I started; and then he seemed to smile.

I could not think him dead – but his face and throat were washed with rain; the bedclothes dripped, and he was perfectly still. The lattice, flapping to and fro, had grazed one hand that rested on the sill; no blood trickled from the broken skin, and when I put my fingers to it, I could doubt no more: he was dead and stark!

I hasped the window; I combed his black long hair from his forehead; I tried to close his eyes: to extinguish, if possible, that frightful, lifelike gaze of exultation before anyone else beheld it. They would not shut: they seemed to sneer at my attempts; and his parted lips and sharp white teeth sneered too! Taken with another fit of cowardice, I cried out for Joseph. Joseph shuffled up and made a noise, but resolutely refused to meddle with him.

'Th' divil's harried off his soul,' he cried, 'and he may hev' his carcass into t'bargin, for aught I care! Ech! What a wicked 'un he looks, girning at death!' and the old sinner grinned in mockery.

I thought he intended to cut a caper round the bed; but suddenly composing himself, he fell on his knees, and raised his hands, and returned thanks that the lawful master and the ancient stock were restored to their rights.

I felt stunned by the awful event; and my memory unavoidably recurred to former times with a sort of oppressive sadness. But poor Hareton, the most wronged, was the only one who really suffered much. He sat by the corpse all night, weeping in bitter earnest. He pressed its hand, and kissed the sarcastic, savage face that everyone else shrank from contemplating; and bemoaned him with that strong grief which springs naturally from a generous heart, though it be tough as tempered steel.

Kenneth was perplexed to pronounce of what disorder the master died. I concealed the fact of his having swallowed nothing for four days, fearing it might lead to trouble, and then, I am persuaded, he did not abstain on purpose: it was the consequence of his strange illness, not the cause.

We buried him, to the scandal of the whole neighbourhood, as he wished. Earnshaw and I, the sexton, and six men to carry the coffin, comprehended the whole attendance.

The six men departed when they had let it down into the grave: we stayed to see it covered. Hareton, with a streaming face, dug green sods, and laid them over the brown mould himself: at present it is as smooth and verdant as its companion mounds – and I hope its tenant sleeps as soundly. But the country folks, if you ask them, would swear on the Bible that he *walks*: there are those who speak to having met him near the church, and on the moor, and even within this house. Idle tales, you'll say, and so say I. Yet that old man by the kitchen fire affirms he has seen two on 'em looking out of his chamber window on every rainy night since his death: – and an odd thing happened to me about a month ago.

I was going to the Grange one evening – a dark evening, threatening thunder – and, just at the turn of the Heights, I encountered a little boy with a sheep and two lambs before him; he was crying terribly; and I supposed the lambs were skittish, and would not be guided.

'What is the matter, my little man?' I asked.

'There's Heathcliff and a woman yonder, under

t'nab,' he blubbered, 'un I darnut pass 'em. I saw nothing; but neither the sheep nor he would go on so I bid him take the road lower down. He probably raised the phantoms from thinking, as he traversed the moors alone, on the nonsense he had heard his parents and companions repeat. Yet, still, I don't like being out in the dark now; and I don't like being left by myself in this grim house: I cannot help it; I shall be glad when they leave it, and shift to the Grange!

'They are going to the Grange, then?' I said.*

'Yes,' answered Mrs. Dean, 'as soon as they are married, and that will be on New Year's Day.'

'And who will live here then?'

'Why, Joseph will take care of the house, and, perhaps, a lad to keep him company. They will live in the kitchen, and the rest will be shut up.'

'For the use of such ghosts as choose to inhabit it?' I observed.

'No, Mr. Lockwood,' said Nelly, shaking her head. 'I believe the dead are at peace: but it is not right to speak of them with levity.'

At that moment the garden gate swung to; the ramblers were returning.

'*They* are afraid of nothing,' I grumbled, watching their approach through the window. 'Together, they would brave Satan and all his legions.'

As they stepped on to the door stones, and halted

* 'They' in this case are Hareton and young Catherine Linton, both of whom we met in the first extract in this book.

to take a last look at the moon – or, more correctly, at each other by her light – I felt irresistibly impelled to escape them again; and, pressing a remembrance into the hand of Mrs. Dean, and disregarding her expostulations at my rudeness, I vanished through the kitchen as they opened the house door; and so should have confirmed Joseph in his opinion of his fellow servant's gay indiscretions, had he not fortunately recognised me for a respectable character by the sweet ring of a sovereign at his feet.

My walk home was lengthened by a diversion in the direction of the kirk. When beneath its walls, I perceived decay had made progress, even in seven months: many a window showed black gaps deprived of glass; and slates jutted off here and there, beyond the right line of the roof, to be gradually worked off in coming autumn storms.

I sought, and soon discovered, the three headstones on the slope next the moor: the middle one grey, and half buried in the heath; Edgar Linton's only harmonized by the turf and moss creeping up its foot; Heathcliff's still bare.

I lingered round them, under that benign sky: watched the moths fluttering among the heath and harebells, listened to the soft wind breathing through the grass, and wondered how anyone could ever imagine unquiet slumbers for the sleepers in that quiet earth.

✠ One encounters all manner of 'unquiet' beings – comical and menacing in varying degrees – in the two great novels of the Irish writer Flann O'Brien, *At-Swim-Two-Birds* (1939) and *The Third Policeman* (written between 1939–1940, but not published until 1967). The newspaper column he wrote for many years in the *Irish Times*, under the pseudonym Myles na gCopaleen, features many dazzling examples of how to find the fantastical in everyday life; but it also contains this story of an encounter with something far more disturbing – as well as suggesting an intriguing alternative way of facing down 'evil machinations'.

Flann O'Brien

– Cruiskeen Lawn column, *Irish Times*, 4 December 1944 –

M any years ago a Dublin friend asked me to spend an evening with him. Assuming that the man was interested in philosophy and knew that immutable truth can sometimes be acquired through the kinesis of disputation, I consented. How wrong I was may be judged from the fact that my friend arrived at the rendezvous in a taxi and whisked me away to a licensed premises in the vicinity of Lucan. Here I was induced to consume a large measure of intoxicating whiskey. My friend would not hear of another drink in the same place, drawing my attention by nudges to a very sinister-looking character who was drinking stout in the shadows some distance from us. He was a tall cadaverous person, dressed wholly in black, with a face of deathly grey. We left and drove many miles to the village of Stepaside, where a further drink was ordered. Scarcely to the lip had it been applied when both of us noticed – with what feelings I dare not describe – the same tall creature in black, residing in a distant shadow and apparently drinking the same glass of stout. We finished our own drinks quickly and left at once, taking in this case the Enniskerry road and entering a hostelry in the purlieus of that village. Here more drinks were ordered but had hardly appeared on the counter when, to the horror of myself and friend, the sinister stranger was discerned some distance away, still patiently dealing with his stout. We swallowed our drinks raw and hurried out. My friend was now thoroughly scared, and could not be dissuaded from making for the far-away hamlet of Celbridge; his idea was that, while another drink was absolutely essential, it was equally essential to put as many miles as possible between ourselves and the sinister presence we had just left. Need I say what happened? We noticed with relief that the public house we entered in Celbridge was deserted, but as our eyes became more accustomed to the poor light, *we saw him again*; he was standing in the gloom, a more terrible apparition than ever before, ever more menacing with each meeting. My friend had purchased a bottle of whiskey and was now dealing with the stuff in large gulps. I saw at once that a crisis had been reached and that desperate action was called for.

'No matter where we go,' I said, 'this being will be there unless we can now assert a superior will and confound evil machinations that are on foot. I do not know whence comes this apparition, but certainly of this world it is not. It is my intention to challenge him.'

My friend gazed at me in horror, made some gesture of remonstrance, but apparently could not speak. My own mind was made up. It was me or this diabolical adversary: there could be no evading the clash of wills, only one of us could survive. I finished my drink with an assurance I was far from feeling and marched straight up to the presence. A nearer sight of him almost stopped the action of my heart; here undoubtedly was no man but some spectral emanation from the tomb, the undead come on some task of inhuman vengeance.

'I do not like the look of you,' I said, somewhat lamely.

'I don't think so much of you either,' the thing replied; the voice was cracked, low and terrible.

'I demand to know,' I said sternly, 'why you persist in following myself and my friend everywhere we go.'

'I cannot go home until you first go home,' the thing replied. There was an ominous undertone in this that almost paralysed me.

'Why not?' I managed to say.

'Because I am the – taxi-driver!'

Out of such strange incidents is woven the pattern of what I am pleased to call my life.

From *The Best of Myles*, 1987

– ACKNOWLEDGEMENTS –

First and foremost I have to thank Kim Kremer of Notting Hill Editions for suggesting this book and for encouraging me to edit it. I'd also like to thank Lucy Walker of Britten Pears Arts for involving me in her discovery day on Benjamin Britten and Henry James's takes on *The Turn of the Screw*, and for some stimulating conversations on the subject of ghost stories. Lastly I'd like to thank my late mother; her legacy has in many ways been difficult and complicated, but she was also an inspired storyteller. I'm pretty sure telling stories helped her deal with her own internal spectres, and perhaps unwittingly she also pointed the way to me to deal with mine. That certainly was no wrong turning.

– PERMISSIONS –

'Black Dog', a short story from *Pack of Cards* (William Heinemann, 1986) by Penelope Lively, reproduced by kind permission of the author; two extracts from *Moominpapa at Sea* copyright © Tove Jansson, 1965, Moomin Characters™, and English translation copyright © 1950, Moomin Characters™, reproduced with permission of Moomin Characters™; extract from *The Best of Myles* copyright © 1968 by Evelyn O'Nolan, reprinted by permission of HarperCollins Publishers Ltd and Dalkey Archive Press.

Other titles from Notting Hill Editions*

How Shostakovich Changed My Mind
Stephen Johnson

Music broadcaster Stephen Johnson explores the power of
Shostakovich's music and how it gave hope during Stalin's reign
of terror. He writes of the healing effect of music on sufferers
of mental illness and how Shostakovich's music helped him
survive the trials of bipolar disorder.

On Dolls
Edited by Kenneth Gross

The essays in this collection explore the seriousness of play and
the mysteries of inanimate life. Includes contributions from
Baudelaire, Rilke, Kafka and Freud.

Sauntering: Writers Walk Europe
Introduced and Edited by Duncan Minshull

Sauntering features sixty writers – classic and contemporary
– who travel Europe by foot. We join Henriette D'Angeville
climbing Mont Blanc; Nellie Bly roaming the trenches of war-
torn Poland; Werner Herzog on a personal pilgrimage across
Germany; Hans Christian Andersen in quarantine; Joseph
Conrad in Cracow; and Robert Macfarlane dropping deep into
underground Paris.

Still Life with a Bridle
Zbigniew Herbert

The poet Zbigniew Herbert brings the Dutch seventeenth-
century alive: the people, as they bid crippling sums of money
for one bulb of a new variety of tulip, and the painters like
Torrentius who was persecuted for heresy and whose paintings
disappeared – all but one, named *Still Life with a Bridle*.

Frida Kahlo and My Left Leg
Emily Rapp Black

At first sight of Frida Kahlo's famous painting *The Two Fridas*, Emily Rapp Black felt an instant connection with the artist. Like Kahlo, Rapp Black is an amputee who grew up with a succession of prosthetic limbs and learned to hide her disability from the world. Like Kahlo, Rapp Black has lived in a world where non-normative bodies are either not discussed, or are fetishized. In this hugely personal and exhilarating new book, Rapp Black draws on the art, letters and diaries of Kahlo in order to make sense of her own life and body.

What Time Is It?
John Berger & Selcuk Demirel

A profound and playful meditation on the illusory nature of time. Illustrated throughout in full colour by Turkish artist Selcuk Demirel in his inventive style and introduced by Berger's friend Maria Nadotti.

Essays on the Self by Virginia Woolf
Introduced by Joanna Kavenna

In these thirteen essays, Woolf celebrates the urgency of the present; and explores the nature of the finite self ('Who am I?' 'Who is everybody else'?) and how individual experience might be relayed.

Subscribe to our newsletter at nottinghilleditions.com

Treat yourself or a friend to a new book every month with one of our subscription plans at nottinghilleditions.com/subscriptions/

*All titles are available in the UK, and some titles are available in the rest of the world. For more information please visit www.nottinghilleditions.com.

A selection of our titles is distributed in the US and Canada by New York Review Books. For more information on available titles please visit www.nyrb.com